Simply Stallions

Arian Mabe

This is a collection of short stories focusing on erotic encounters with anthro stallions, including three stories with a hippocampus (water horse). Other anthro and human characters are included for variety, with a stallion focus.

This story collection covers gay erotica, oral & anal sex, light BDSM, light domination/submission, exhibitionism and cock/ball worship.

Table of Contents

Worshipping His Rod

There was only one way to please a stud and that was down on my knees, my nose buried into the crease between his nuts. I inhaled deeply, letting my husky nose twitch even closer in between his balls, tongue stroking out, caressing behind them and then up and over in one long sweep.

"Oh, fuck, yes…"

I trembled. Yes. That was what I wanted, the stallion stud above me losing control, though it was not as if Shawn and I had not spent so much time together already that I did not know, intimately, how to please him. In his bedroom, our flats not all that far from one another on the outskirts of a town that had suited us both well enough after university and starting our working lives, I could have told anyone else the placement of every item in there. But all my focus, at that time, was on the glory of the stallion before me.

Shawn was a Shire stallion, his coat dark, though he said he was bay. To my eye, it was almost black, but the long, white feather that spilt down around his fetlocks and hooves was what I truly adored. My paws slid gently down his thick, tree-trunk-like thighs, caressing him lightly, though the stallion could take far, far more than me. I was just a husky, after all, a good head and shoulders shorter than Shawn, if not more. But my tail curled up in just the right way to catch the eye of the studs that I wanted to take home with me.

Somehow, I always ended up back with Shawn. As if there was a bond between us, something more than a casual fling, a friends-with-benefits gig, that kept me coming back to him, again and again.

One day, I would have to investigate that further, but, in that moment, all I had to do was to be pleasing to him – and to enjoy.

My tongue dipped languidly into his sheath, toying with it, how the fleshy fold moved back and forth, not quite snug around the base of his cock. Shawn was thick, but not so thick that it caused problems with his sheath, and I smirked as I peeled it back a little, all to caress parts of his cock with my tongue that did not usually get such intimate attention. He grunted and stomped, a hand stroking my head, the flaring red of my fur before it blurred into soft white, but the moment was not about me. It was all about my worship of him, trailing my tongue up his cock, from the very base that I'd exposed, where his sheath had been a moment ago.

Shawn's heavy breathing hitched and my heart leapt. Oh, how I loved having that effect on him, all as I dragged my tongue slowly up the full length of his cock. It was a long member, a true testament to his equine heritage, long enough that, if I had cared to do so, I could have paused halfway to consider what I was doing and still had a good amount of stallion flesh left to devour. But I didn't stop, not until my tongue bumped over the medial ring and tickled to the tip, swirling around the flare.

"Ah, Kyle…"

It was my name and one of the sweetest things, bar a moan, that I could have heard from his lips. It drove me on to do more, using my lips on the fleshy head of his cock, flat and flared already as if he was about to cum. But I knew something others did not and, even when he was in the middle of a session, the stallion's flare was hot and engorged, dripping and drooling, all as if he was on that very point of orgasm.

It gave me more than plenty to play with as I lapped over it, teasing the sensitive flesh, knowing Shawn could take it. The stallion's fingers tried to curl into the fur on my head, but I did not have hair or a mane like his and there was a lack of things there for him to grab. My cock swelled to attention between my legs from its half-hard state, but I did not mind that, even if it was a rather open, forward sign of just how much I was enjoying worshipping his cock and balls too.

My lips parted over the head of his cock, suckling him into my mouth, relishing the stretch. And yet my paws could not remain idle, not even in a moment like that, sliding up his inner thighs to part them just a little more, to get to the delectable hanging fruit of his balls. They trembled with the shift of his body, cradled within his sack, and I caressed it delicately, keeping the short claws at the tips of my fingers out of the way. I always kept them smooth and filed, but to catch someone's crown jewels with those, well… There were certainly few other ways to spoil the mood quite that quickly.

"Ah, fuck…"

I stroked his balls, pressing the flat of my thumbs into them. I knew just how much pressure to give, for the stallion was far more sensitive down there than he let on. That was just something that came with time spent with a partner, even if I would never have considered Shawn as anything more than a friends-with-benefits kind of partner. Maybe that was my downfall, maybe I should have made a move earlier.

Despite his cock, his throbbing member and seemingly swollen balls – that was just the way they naturally were – my attention remained fixed upon him. I couldn't think of anything else, anyone else, not when I was with him. Despite his glorious body, I knew there was so much more to Shawn than that.

But he deserved all the attention I could give him, sliding down his cock, taking him into my mouth, careful of my teeth. We were, in a sense, predator and prey – but I never felt as small as I did when I was taking him, when I was giving Shawn all the pleasure that I thought I could possibly give. My tongue had to press flat, practically shoved out of the way of his mighty member, but I did not mind that, not as he pressed on my head, begging me to go deeper. Yet Shawn was not a rough sort, the kind of stallion who wanted me to go at my own pace, despite his own need.

Something warmed in me at that and I groaned around him, letting the vibrations travel from my lips down into his cock, giving him a little extra sensation, all that I could tease him with, please him with.

I bobbed my head on his cock, feeling him press into my throat as I gulped, wanting that length. I wanted him to press deeper, though it still made my eyes water, even as I did my best to suppress my gag reflex. The thickness of his cock in my throat made me want to gag even as my aching shaft throbbed, harder than ever and leaking pre-cum. Oh, I wanted it, even if it was uncomfortable for me – but didn't the best kinds of sex come with that tiny edge of discomfort? Not everything was meant to be smooth and warm and seamless in sex. It was those gritty edges of reality that made it all the hotter to me, not just a fantasy but something tangible that I could reach out and take for my own.

I took him deep, letting the hot length of horse dick slide down my throat, despite the pressure. I loved the pressure, the feel of his bulge, the need of him, how his flare thickened even further within my throat. Even though I wanted to spend my time and attention on adoring and worshipping his nuts too, I had to concentrate, eyes closed, taking his cock as far down my stretched throat as possible.

Gulping around him, I moaned, sliding back and forth, bobbing my head, desire twisting and curling in the base of my loins. My cock ached, but the attention was not there to give at that moment, suckling on his cock, lips pursing as I drooled around him. I wanted more, so much more, that heady, slick load of horse cum pouring down my throat. Already, I could feel, in my recollection, just how his cock would pulse in my mouth while spending his seed, how much would fill my mouth, bubbling out of the corners of my lips even when I tried to swallow it all down. Sometimes, even a husky was not as good as they might have liked to be at drinking down the best kind of treat, better than fine wine.

Not that I drank much wine, but, oh well…

It was as good an analogy as I was going to come up with as I groaned around him, drawing back, a string of pre-cum and saliva clinging to his cock, dangling to my lips. I moaned, lapping over the head with the flat side of my tongue, though his nuts were where I belonged, sliding back down and holding his cock above my head with both paws.

They stroked up and down, ensuring that every inch of his throbbing shaft got the same attention, every last little bit of the attention that it deserved, my nose caressing his nuts. The thick meat of his cock filled my paws perfectly, even though he was technically more horse than I could handle, lips parting and moaning before I could stop myself.

"Shawn… Come on, stud, I know you've got it in you, you're so fucking close… Cum for me, come on."

I was practically begging him, all without thinking, jacking him off furiously as if there was nothing else in the whole world that I could have wanted more, fingers sliding over the medial ring. And the beautiful stud of a stallion gave me everything that I could ever have dreamed of and so much more, bellowing as he stomped, tail lashing the air in a thick swish of hair.

Cum erupted over my head, spurting, splattering everywhere, pouring down over my head as if I was taking a very kinky kind of shower. It was where I belonged, cock throbbing, though my orgasm was not yet to be taken. Not as I languished there, adoring him, Shawn's cum in my mouth, drooling over my head, the rich scent of his stallion musk heavy in my nostrils. His balls jostled against my face as Shawn could not help but thrust and grind, losing control, but I didn't need him to have control when I was there to contain it for him.

It was up to me to devour his load, pushing back to the head of his cock, slurping, lapping, drooling, though the mess was entirely down to me, even if it came from the stallion's cock. That meant nothing, not when I was the one that had caused the entire "issue," my tail wagging furiously as I took as much down my throat as I could.

I needed it, perhaps more than him, the stallion giving great, heaving pants, tail flagging proudly with the head of his cock incredibly flared, so thick and so fleshy. I moaned, trying to part my lips far enough to get his flare into my mouth, sucking down as much of him as I could. But with his flare engorged to that extent, I couldn't do as I wished, forced to let his cum paint my muzzle, neck and bare chest – and wherever the hell else his cum went – soaking into my fur.

Worshipping his cock and balls was the best thing that I could think of to do, even if there was more to our relationship than that. It was there if I wanted to take it, smiling as I looked up at Shawn, licking off my lips, though it was a futile effort indeed, considering the amount of cum drooling down me.

I took a deep breath. It was okay. I could do it. I needed a shower anyway.

"Maybe I could spend the night?"

It was about small steps, after all.

Servicing the Stallions

The tiger swayed on his knees, the stable cast into a shuddering, buzzing, flickering light. The lighting strips overhead needed work or, perhaps, that was just an effect that they used to make everything seem seedier and darker than it actually was, alternating between lighting up the centre aisle of the stables and the stacks of straw laid out just so, at the side. His blue fur bristled, the darker stripes slashed through starkly, but Tanner could not even breathe, chest rising and falling swiftly as he squirmed in bondage that, perhaps, he had accepted just a little too readily.

Ah, well... There was no matter for that anymore and only so very much to look forward to. Mewling softly, he turned his head from one side to the other, paws bound behind his back and thighs to his calves, while he knelt there. He could tip over, if he wanted to, but that would have put his muzzle too far down to truly do what he was there for, panting heavily even as his eyes wantonly rolled back into his skull, tail flicking anxiously back and forth, although it was not the only outward demonstration of desire he gave.

The black stallion who had brought him there loomed, a tall, imposing figure with folded arms, taking his time even as a slow, easy smirk spread across his soft, equine lips. Just the one white sock reached up over his bare fetlock, resting his weight back lightly on his hocks as he nickered keenly, tail swishing in a slow, steady, hypnotising cut of the air.

Swish.

Swish

Swish.

Tanner sucked in a breath, eyes wide, and yet words would not leap to his lips as that length of stallion-meat grew right there before his muzzle, a throbbing girth of pink and grey, the skin wrinkled where it had not yet quite fleshed out with divine blood.

For that was the need that every stallion required in the end, was it not? The lust of the body coming to carnal fruition in the most lustful of ways was what every stud sought and he'd found just the right little submissive kitty-cat to satisfy his every last need.

Snorting, he stomped a hoof, not even bothering to grope and squeeze his own shaft, for the sight of his little, bound toy for the night got him hard and ready for anything, as quick as he would like. He'd only worn a loincloth, leaving every last inch of his studly, muscled glory, coat shining with good health, on show.

"You know why you're here..."

Heart pounding, all he could do was nod as that that god of a stallion slipped down his loincloth, casting it aside so that there was no longer anything concealing the raging rod of growing stallion meat – not that such a puny slip of cloth could have hoped to hide it anyway. And, as if in a dream, the length of horse meat pushed towards his lips, forcing them open with the drooling, flat tip as if the stud stallion simply could not contain himself. And just why would he ever have possibly had to hold back? Groaning around him, the tiger flattened his ears lightly back to his head and took everything he could, pressing his rough tongue up to the underside, savouring every bit of the horse that he could in the heat of the moment. And yet that was something that proved more difficult, perhaps, than it should have been, tongue rasping along the length as the equine stud quickly and surely bottomed out in the back of his throat.

But that wasn't going to satisfy a stud who was well enough used to having his every need met and Tanner was well and truly stuck, encircled by anthro horses that seemed to appear from everywhere. Had he just not noticed them before? Or had he just been so wrapped up in the lusty wiles of one that he had excluded all else to the lustful grind and hump of his cock? It didn't matter, not at all, but what did matter was how that shaft demanded more, deeper, all the while. He was too small! Or at least he would have tried to say that if his mouth wasn't stuffed full of horse cock, hacking and gagging on that hot length even as his eyes watered.

And, still...there was a part of him that wanted to feel the grunting stallion's crotch shoved up against his flat little nose, as deep as he could possibly go. He didn't have the long muzzle of an equine, after all, and could only do what his body allowed him to – not that the stallion was going to take any kind of no or complaint for an answer, however. He leaned over Tanner with feral glee, a heady snort bursting from his nostrils as he forced the tiger down and down and down, for there were so many others who also needed his pleasure. The other stallions nickered and clamoured for the attention of their newest slut tiger, stroking raging, hard cocks with large paws that didn't even properly fit around their fat lengths, each one offering something new and different from the one that came previously.

Inhaling shallowly, the tiger cried out, eyes half-lidded with lust. Pain blurred into a stream of pleasure, his dick hard and yet denied any sense of pleasure as much as he humped and ground his hips. He had been brought there, after all, to service the stallions and no one would exactly care all that much for the needs of a cat on his knees, which he well enough knew. That didn't stop his hips from grinding, rocking as if he was imagining just how it would feel to have the paw of one of the studs wrapped around his cock, jacking him off to a crude yet blissful climax.

But the stallion had no desire to last forever and, too quickly, Tanner's eyes shot open, the stud's nuts pulling up, churning urgently, in the prelude to climax. And, when it came, it came in a deluge of thick cum, pouring straight down the tiger's throat as his ear was pinched and his head dragged all the way down whether he liked it or not, although the throbbing of his dripping shaft told a tale that his lips could not.

Moaning around that hot length, the cum-vein pulsing and throbbing delightfully, he dutifully drank down every drop, savouring the musky taste, the slickness of it, as the black stallion drew back a little, spending the last spurts (as virile as they still were) on to his tongue as if to demonstrate his claim. Tanner cried out softly, lips and tongue working to clean that shaft of every last drop of semen and fluid that the stud had to offer, lost in a delirium of his own lust from which he very much doubted he'd find any such escape from. And that was just the way that Tanner wanted to be, just so he could be in his rightful place.

Shuddering, the stallion's tail lifted, exposing the underside of the dock as something in his gut tightened, a different kind of need making itself known.

"Unnff..."

Yet one orgasm was not all that the stallions had to offer as Tanner was hefted up on to a bale of straw, a stallion who he only saw as a flash of reddish-brown hair pinning him to slam too easily up into his tail hole, which had already been prepared with a liberal (rather kind) helping of lubricant. If he hadn't had that much, well, he could only imagine just how much that first thrust would have hurt but there was little he could have done to avoid it, squirming in his bondage and gulping around another cock, this time belonging to a palomino stud with pure pink flesh on his length. It was all the same to the tiger who swallowed him down without question, the lingering taste of musky semen in his mouth mingling with fresh dick as he was fucked from both ends, left still wanting more as his cock ground into the straw beneath his body.

More… So much more. Stallion after stallion passed him off, turning him over on to his back and spending liberal, voluminous loads of cum on to his stomach, marking his own shaft even as he cried out, brokenly, around another fat length of horse meat, forced into orgasm with just a crude finger rammed up under his tail, just to prove their dominance over him. He was nothing more than a toy that could be passed around between them for their pleasure, one covering him after another, the heady and intoxicating aroma of lusty bodies and cum flooding the barn like nothing else could, the earthen scent of the horses themselves near enough overpowering.

Yet what could one tiger do as he was lifted into the air, a cock squeezing into his tail hole (the largest yet belonging to a red Percheron stud), forcing him open even as he yowled and jetted out a comparatively weak orgasm before the watching, mocking equines? No, there was nothing he could do or even wanted to do to end his sweet debasement, hay tickling his nose and a tail flipping up over his head as his tongue was pressed to a pair of smooth, black nuts, another cock already up in his tail hole as if the one that came before had never left.

One sensation blurred into another as time went on, the sense of time passing subtle and yet impossible to judge, as he was passed about and on, a mere sex toy to be used to satisfy their whims. And yet one cat as he sat back on his knees, trying to strain up to a meaty cock where a droplet of pre-cum clung to the tip, surrounded by a ring of needy cocks and yet finding himself drawn to that one. The grey stud that it belonged to laughed softly and shook his mane off the arch of his neck, looking down imperiously as the muscle in his thighs drew taut with raw power.

"You want some more, kitty? I think you like this…"

It's almost as if he had put himself in just the right place, accepting that stallion's offer in the pub, at the right time – why! Even if it was rather more than the feline thought he could handle, it was right, in the end.

Smirking to himself, Tanner mewled cutely and opened his mouth again for the next load, although only time would tell and the experience of it whether he would be able to take it all down without seed bubbling out from the corners of his lips, choking on their seed.

It was going to be a long night in bondage, yet the tiger relished every second of it…

Cock around the Clock

"Are you sure this is a good idea?"

The stallion snorted softly, blowing his forelock out of his eyes, the black and white draft horse reminiscent of his Vanner heritage, though a typical cob would not have grown as large as he was. His huge, dinnerplate-sized hooves hung off the end of the college dorm bed, though they, for once, had the place to themselves, his boyfriend's roommate out of town for the weekend, visiting family.

Having single-sex dorms for college, adults tasting their first lick of freedom after being in the parental nest for so many years, was a good idea in practice – less so when sexualities other than heterosexual were considered. Yet that was just one place in which those that liked the same sex triumphed (or those that were bi or similar) while straights had to sneak off around campus and off campus just to get a grope and a feel. Of course, the opposite sex was not permitted to be in the dorms themselves, though that didn't stop many that were so inclined from sneaking partners in.

David stretched out on the bed, half-naked with his chest bare, his wolf partner, Samuel or Sam for short, splayed out over his back. The size difference between the wolf and the horse was laughable sometimes, with the wolf being more on the diminutive, effeminate side, though Sam didn't mind that at all. It was just how he was and his sassy flair and confidence had gained him a lot of friends at college so far, living and thriving in dorm life more than some. The horse, however, had not settled as quickly until he'd found him, hooking up for the first time at a party that they really should not have been drinking at, but, oh well. Things like that happened at college and a raging hangover in someone else's bed was merely just one of many rites of passage.

"Hm?" Sam nuzzled the back of his neck, sharp teeth playfully catching at his black mane. "What? Don't you think it'll be fun?"

David blushed and shook his head, the little packet of pills tucked in the palm of his large hand.

"Well… It's Viagra, yeah?" He said, stalling for a moment. "But I don't really need help getting it up, you know… We don't have any issues there."

"Yeahhhh," Sam said, dragging out the word as he slipped off the horse's back to sprawl on the bed. "But it's one…you know, that keeps you *going* too. You know what I mean? You can get it over the counter at the drugstore."

Still, David looked dubious, his ears twitching back and forth while his tail tucked down over his rump, though he was most usually not the one being penetrated, so he had no real reason to demurely hide.

"I mean… They said it's safe, right?"

"Absolutely," Sam said with a typical, wide, toothy wolf grin. "Of course… C'mon, David, I'm not going to give you anything that would be bad for you, you know that."

Of course, David knew that, but things with a guy like Sam with soft fur and a wicked gleam in his eye, always up for another round or something more akin to mischief, were still new to him. Yet, in a way, that made everything with the grey wolf even more exciting than it could have been if he had been a more seasoned, experienced lover, something that David did not mind in the slightest.

Undoubtedly, they were both there at college to study, but the relaxation in the infatuation of Sam's lips, the wolf shrugging out of his vest top, sleeveless, of course, and kissing him warmly, tangling with him on top of the bedsheets… Mmm… There was something about that, something that kept the draft horse coming back for more, his protests softening and slipping away with a needy nicker.

He didn't need it, but the wolf's hand groped and massaged his sheath through his jeans anyway, hands fumbling, teasing, the edge of inexperience still floating between them. Whereas they were both in the prime of their sexual lives, there was only so much experience that could be safely gained so quickly and it was all something that they wanted to take their time with, just to have fun. They were boyfriends, but…no more than that had been said.

Clothes left bodies hardened with lust, the wolf's shaft easing from his sheath, David's head swirling with passion. It did that when all the blood in his body seemed to rush from his brain to far more alluring parts, his thick cock throbbing, fleshing up and out in a fat spill of stallion flesh.

"Mmmm…" Sam dropped, naked on the bed with him, nuzzling the base of the horse's cock and running his tongue up and over the medial ring, tasting him. "You're so fucking hot… Go on, take it… I want to really see you destroy my ass tonight."

David winced, though he couldn't help the tiniest of smirks. Damn that wolf… Was he ever not randy? He swore Sam could go all night and go again, while he, to be fair, often wanted to crash out after a couple of rounds, which was, for most, par for the course. He could still cum like a fire hydrant – or at least that was how the wolf often described it – but sometimes that wasn't enough for a partner. The spice of life was experimentation…er…or something like that, the horse thought.

It was hard to think clearly while the wolf took his cock into his maw, well-used to keeping his teeth carefully back and away from his partner's dick. It was not an easy feat and something that had led to scraping and accidents in the earlier days of their relationship, but that was hardly something that David had in mind.

He moaned, scrambling for one of the pills, a little blue round that looked so innocent. Again, even as his dick disappeared hotly into the wet, lashing warmth of the wolf's maw, he checked the packet, but it looked like a normal Viagra, even if it could "make him go all night" as the wolf said. He'd always thought that Viagra was just to help guys get it up, not to fuck for longer, but who was he to say?

"Unff… To hell with it…"

He downed the pill, tossing his head back as he fell to his back on the bed, the old, creaky mattress protesting at such rough treatment. The wolf came right along with him, pushing down on his cock, head bobbing, tail wagging, lifting already like the needy little pup he was. Sam had been teasing at getting David to call him "nastier names," like telling him how slutty he was, but David still couldn't see why at all Sam would want to be demeaned like that. But maybe they'd get there, one day, the wolf's lips so soft, so sweet, so tender on his aching, throbbing hard-on.

He didn't know how long the pill would take to affect him, but that was none of his concern, not as he swallowed, his large hands with hoof-like, rough tips to his fingers landing on the back of Sam's head. The pull of the wolf's throat at the overly sensitive tip of his cock was too intoxicating to pass up, how slick his tongue was over his smooth flesh, the length of his cock more grey than pink but with a fair amount of splotching still. If they had been in a better position, he would have been jacking off the wolf too, making sure that he gave as much as he got, even though Sam liked to devour him more than to actually receive.

"God, Sam," he hissed out through his teeth, gritting them together, still not wanting to cum too quickly. "Fuck... That feels good... So...good..."

David only swore when he was getting head or having sex and, well, he didn't want anyone other than Sam to hear him using such crude language. He rolled his hips up, cock aching, his balls churning, the heaviness of his nuts seeming to make them swell, so fat and so ready, even then. He, of course, knew that was not possible, yet the strain and the pushing feeling of need deep within his gut had to be made sense of one way or another in his mind.

Yet his mind was not working as well as it could have been in that moment, his entire body aching, legs trembling and kicking up the bedsheets as he tried to get his knees up. There was no one quite like Sam to make him weak at the knees, however, the wolf's lips sliding down over his medial ring, sucking lightly, his cheeks even hollowing while his agile, flexible tongue worked over the underside in long, lustful laps.

"Ah... Yes... God..."

David scrabbled, trying to hold on to himself, his ears slipping back, trying not to lose control too quickly, but he couldn't help it. The wolf gulped around the head of his cock, the flare thickening within his mouth, eyes dancing and tail lifting with obvious glee. Yet the horse was in quite the predicament, cock throbbing, every pulse of blood making it harder, closer to the edge, so sensitive that he thought he couldn't hold back for a single moment more.

"Unff... Fuck!" David cursed, heat rushing to his cheeks and ears, creeping hotly down his neck. "Gonna... Fuck, Sam, can't go that hard... Gonna cum..."

But the wolf only took that as a challenge, diving all the way down on his cock, as far as he could go, a fat bulge showing through Sam's throat. He could not swallow everything down, not yet anyway, not with a gag reflex, but he could keep trying, eyes watering, whimpering, whining with pure lust, simply wanting more and more, aching for it. And David was along for the ride, one way or another, the soft, trembling vibrations of the wolf moaning around his cock travelling deep into him.

He couldn't hold it, trying to get his hips up as high as he could and failing dismally, though it did not feel like a failure at all as thick ropes of seed flooded the wolf's muzzle. Like the cock sucking pro Sam had become, the wolf gulped it all down without allowing a single drop to escape, though the case would not be such later in the night, the student nightlife brimming over outside their dorm window.

All David could do was let pleasure wash through him, each throb of cum coming with another wave of ecstasy, stronger than ever, though he would still lament that his lust did not last as long as it could. There were things, apparently, that a guy could do to make his orgasm last longer, but David had not looked into them more than hearing that, collapsing back on the bed, his sheath feeling tighter around the base of his cock than it usually did.

Yet, that time, his eyelids did not droop as they would have before, the horse rumbling softly in the back of his throat as if he had become a more predatory species, sitting up a moment later. He was too awake, too invigorated, Sam's eyes wide as he drew back off his cock, the wolf's tail lifting hopefully.

"Did it kick in yet?"

If the tingling vitality and what had to be virility aching passionately through every bone and every vein in his body meant that the pill, Cock around the Clock, had kicked in – that was a resounding *yes*. The horse gulped, but he couldn't help himself, not as the wolf tumbled laughing into his arms, their hard-ons grinding together, rolling back and forth on the bed.

Oh, it was a good feeling, a very good feeling, his cock sensitive but his body still wanting more, to the point that he felt that he could push past that sensitivity. And maybe that was exactly what Sam had been wanting from him the whole time, wanting to find out what it was that the stallion needed so that he could break free to the next level in sex, not holding back for any reason, not from shyness or anything that had no place between them, not in their relationship.

David moaned, pinning the wolf down on his belly, the stallion on top of him, cock grinding between his ass cheeks and smearing pre-cum into his tail as if it already knew where to go. His flare had not softened as much as usual, but that was of no worry to either of them, not even as Sam's breath hitched and he glanced back, a hint of trepidation in his face for the first time.

"Fuck… David…" He licked the horse's cum from the side of his muzzle, where an errant drip had been smeared, the taste of stallion still thick in his mouth. "You're so…big… Your flare… Ah!"

Yet David wasn't waiting as he gave the wolf exactly what he wanted, using the slick lubrication that his shaft produced to grind tenaciously into the wolf's rump. Inch after inch disappeared inside the wolf, the stallion only in control enough to stop himself from roughly ramming him full. Of course, Sam might well have liked that, but hurting his partner in the heat of the moment would have led to a very pleasureless night for David.

But he couldn't help himself, the wolf's moans music to his ears, still making him want to fuck him harder and faster, sliding in past the medial ring as Sam squirmed delightedly on his dick. Even if he loved it, there was still nowhere for the wolf to go, not as he humped and ground back against David's length, aching for more. Impaled on his cock as he was, all Sam could do was submit to it, tongue lolling pinkly from his muzzle, whimpering and grunting, not even able to form any manner of sensible words.

"Mmm... Ah!"

The stallion snorted, nostrils flaring and puckering, thrusting, grinding, finding ways to get his cock deeper and deeper, though the draw back for every thrust was perhaps the sweetest of all. His body eagerly anticipated the rush of pleasure when he slammed back inside, wanting it even more, his skin aching and tingling, the black of his coat gleaming in a faint sheen of sweat that could not be seen as easily on the white. His mane clung to the dampness of his neck, heat flooding his body, balls aching, bouncing very faintly off the wolf's backside as David held him down, forcing his partner to grind his own cock into the bed.

The wolf cried out passionately, though David could not be sure if he climaxed or not, too far gone with the pulsing lust of vitality coursing through him. If he'd known that taking Cock around the Clock could make him feel so good, give so much to David... He moaned loudly, suddenly not caring who heard him. Damn, if he'd known that, he would have taken the pill when Sam suggested it a long time ago.

Yet the pleasure of Cock around the Clock was still to be seen as the stallion lusciously took his pleasure, revelling in the succulent tightness of the wolf's backside around him. Sam clenched as if he was trying to make the horse's job even more difficult than it already was, but he could still thrust, grunting, his hands on Sam's shoulders, holding him down into the bed while the wolf cried out his name.

"Unff… David!" He gasped, eyes half-closed, tail yanked well up out of the way. "Oh, fuck, yes… Harder… Please!"

David didn't have a say in the matter, the roll and thrust of his body dictated by the wolf and the pill, desperate for it. He'd only just cum, but, already, he had to cum again, his flare still fat and full, his body tricked into thinking that it had even more to spend than usual. His balls would be milked dry by the wolf's tail hole and mouth by the end of the night, but the two of them would see the dawn easily by the time the pill wore off, he was sure of it. Maybe a couple more rounds?

The stallion almost did not care how many rounds they took in their entirety, only that the throb of orgasm, once again coursing through him, was so sweet. David couldn't remember the last time he had cum that quickly, but it didn't matter, nothing else mattered but the heat of the wolf, grinding back on him like he really was… really was…

"Such a slutty wolf," he growled, heat tingling into his ears as he said it, though the rush of warmth running through his cock was even more so potent for it. "You… Unff… Need this…"

And he did, the wolf panting heavily, humping and grinding to the extent that the weight of the equine's body on top of him allowed, though he was too lost in the moment to care about anything else. The stallion did not soften in the slightest as he poured his second load of cum that night straight up the wolf's backside.

Still, to the stallion, it did not feel as if he had cum at all, still thrusting, heaving, grunting and panting, need coursing through him increasingly with every stroke. There was no easing nor any satisfying of his lust, not in any way that he could tell, thrusting harder and faster, hitching the wolf under him up on to his hands and knees.

"Ah… Ah, fuck…" Sam sucked in a breath that was sorely needed. "Yes… Damien… Give me…all…of it…everything…"

He could barely form any coherent words, let alone full sentences, though Damien did not care, leaning over him, covering the wolf's small body with his, easily dwarfing him. Frankly, it was a wonder that his cock fit inside him at the best of times, but he had never gone as deep as he was that day, ramming in hard and fast now that Sam was slick and loosened up for him, balls bouncing off the wolf's own and his backside with every thrust. The light slap, for the equine's nuts were not furred like the wolf's, echoed through the room, though nothing could truly overrule the tenor of their moans.

They should have been quieter than they were, more aware of the risk of getting caught, but college students, even if they were adults, simply didn't care as much about that as they should. All that mattered was lust and Damien's attention had certainly narrowed to that as he sank the entire length of his meat into Sam's vulnerable tail hole.

Their cries tangled, but it was no time at all before the horse fell prey to the pulse of another orgasm, too caught up in what was happening to even be amazed that he was able to cum again so quickly. It didn't feel right that he could get off again so swiftly and yet he did and he could, panting, heaving, thrusting deeper and deeper. Sure, his dick was still sensitive after his third orgasm, but he was so full of energy that he simply couldn't turn down the chance to keep going, to keep thrusting, grinding deeper and deeper.

Of course, he couldn't go much deeper than he already was, though Sam encouraged him on with little whimpers and whines, even as the horse slammed in harder still. The slap of his hips on the wolf's furry rump filled the room, stifling Sam into grunting gasps, eyes closed, his torso tipped down to the bed as he submissively pushed his backside up. His pink cock was exposed, the knot fully inflated, aching on the edge of orgasm even then, though Damien was not to tell that. As long as Sam was still getting every thrust and every drop that he needed, the stallion was more than happy with himself, swishing his tail passionately.

"Unff... Yes... You're so tight still... Mmmph!"

Sam couldn't help himself, pulling the wolf with him, up and back, though the force of gravity pulled the wolf down a touch further on his cock as he managed to wrangle them back into a sitting position, the stallion's legs awkwardly spread. But he could wrap his arms tightly around the wolf's chest in such a position, pulling his fluffy back to his short-haired chest, strong and broad with muscle, pumping him up and down on his cock.

Sam whimpered, head falling back, jaw slack, losing himself, used like a sex toy – but that was just what his mate had promised from Cock around the Clock. It was, apparently, what a guy "really needed" to be pounded all through the night with a raw edge of animalistic passion: what wasn't to like? The wolf only hoped that Damien would keep a few of the new twists and spoils of what they had learned during that night of fun for when the Viagra wore off.

Maybe... But whatever they did keep for themselves would be true to them, their kind of fun, what they enjoyed the most. That was the most important thing, between them, after all.

Another orgasm pumped up into the wolf, but he could not cum, not even as his prostate was lusciously abused. His tapered cock jerked and twitched, drooling pre-cum, but it was nothing in comparison to the heady load of cum slopping up inside his stretched, messy tail hole, the flare of the stallion digging deeply up into him. Damien held him close, somehow managing to shift up on to his knees, but even his energy, in part, had to fade sooner or later.

Energy, yes, but not the hardness of his cock, needing it still. He couldn't control it, making it soften, but he could slip down to the bed, cradling their sweaty bodies together and spooning the wolf as he thrust in longer, more patient strokes. Damien's shoulders rolled back with pleasure, panting and snorting, nostrils flaring for snatches of breath that did not help as much as they could have, need curling tight in the pit of his stomach, a contraction of muscles that he never had thought about before.

Long and slow, but still with need, still with passion, yes. There was more to take, even as he coaxed the wolf to orgasm with his hand around his cock, Sam whimpering through it, though yet another load was added to Sam's backside too. With a plumper lower abdomen than when they had begun, Sam slipped off the horse's cock to a nicker of protest, cleaning them off briefly, before setting to work pumping and sucking the stallion with paws and maw.

Long and slow, despite their exhaustion, their need was more potent than that. For all Sam wanted to be was a little submissive slut, a whore to be used, but in the best of ways, the way where his partner still loved him and curled up around him afterwards. He took load after load into his muzzle, even after the stallion moaned that he didn't have anything left in him anymore, that Cock around the Clock had to be wearing off sooner or later, but the two of them could never have anticipated just how potent it was.

"Around the clock" most certainly was right, for it was with a still hard and aching prick that Damien collapsed around five in the morning, dick throbbing, the wolf of his heart cradled warmly in his arms.

The next morning, too early for any self-respecting student to be awake, the key turned in the door to Sam's room, opening on to the sight of the horse and the wolf curled up together, sheets under them, soaked with cum, Damien's cock still hard. Blinking blearily, the stallion half-lifted his hand, shielding his face from the sudden burst of light and gasp that rose from the other side of the threshold.

"Jesus Christ!" The ferret yelled, slamming the door, red in the face and dropping his bags on the floor. "Put a fucking sock on the doorknob, would you?"

Inside, David groaned, burying his face into the wolf's chest. Sam smirked, his grey tail wagging faintly.

"Hey, looks like Dan's back!"

"Yeah," came David's muffled voice from Sam's chest, buried in his fluff. "I guessed."

It wasn't quite the first time that the horse and the wolf had been walked in during sex and it most certainly would not be the last, considering the height of their lust. They simply lusted for and longed for one another too much to set things aside entirely, handsy and stealing kisses and gropes whenever they thought no one was looking. Young love was that way, at least for them, though they would forever be grateful that they had gone to study in a place that let them experience that.

It was a good few hours, however, before David's cock softened and a red, snapping ferret was allowed back into the room, allowing the draft horse to make good his escape.

One thing was certain… "Cock around the Clock" wasn't a stimulant for the faint of heart!

For the Love of Horse Cock

"Hey there, slut."

I shiver. I know him but I don't know him, a meaty, brawny stud of a stallion with a bay coat and a dark black mane and tail, thick and roughly kept. There is no silken softness to any of them, not when I meet him for the first time in the gym or any time after that, a little rougher around the muzzle too than the guys that I usually dated or hung out with. Sometimes things went further than a date and somethings things ended with a one-night stand, a romp to be remembered. But there is something different about him.

I asked him his name and he said that I didn't need to know. He tossed his gym bag at me, standing, brushing off his shorts, still sweaty and musky. If he'd torn his shirt off right there and then, I would have yanked it to me, cradled it against my chest, shoved it right up over my muzzle and inhaled every last drop of his divinely musky essence that my greedy senses could possibly drink in.

Only, that's not what happened. What happened was that a little black and white stud stallion, if that was what I'd thought of my lightly muscled build in the gym before meeting the beast to reckon with, followed him meekly, got into his car and let the stud drive him away. I knew when I had been beaten and the thickness of his cock slopped obviously from his sheath even as he drove.

Fuck, he is a monster… Back to the present moment, I almost cross my legs in fear of him, neighing shortly, eyes rolling, showing the whites. I shake my head slightly, but he only graces me with a heart-stopping smirk, eyeing me up like a fresh piece of meat to be devoured. The fact that I am a horse, of course, means that it's his cock in my body that will devour me, whether he takes my mouth or my tight tail hole.

I don't know which would be better. I don't know if either would actually be worse in any way. My tail hole tightens and clenches before him as I grunt, though he takes my paw as he drives. There's no saying "no" to him and, with the pound of my heart, I only want to do as he wishes, to obey, snorting, feeling up the massive length of his thickening shaft through his shorts. It's so long that I swear it's about to poke out the leg of his shorts, though maybe that would have not been the case if the stud had been wearing underwear. His thighs are as thick as tree trunks and I can't resist a squeeze, feeling out the masculine, thick shape of him. Beside him, I might as well be scrawny.

"Oh, god…"

"Yeah, slut, that's all for you."

I shake in place, but we're pulling up at what I suspect is his place, my body limply drawn from the car, a puppet being piloted to his will.

Into the house.

Up the stairs.

His lips on mine, tongue claiming my muzzle, sweeping around the interior like my tongue has never done before. He knows every part of me without me even inviting him in and it seems like no time at all before I am down on my knees and naked before him, an equally nude stud stallion who is bigger than me, more masculine than me, better than me in all ways.

Not to mention his dick…

There is nothing more succulent in the whole world than a fresh length of horse cock, a stud's hand curling through my mane. I shudder there, but I know my little prick does not compare to a massive stud's fat meat, even though we are both of the equine variety. My shaft tries to throb and harden, but I can't pay it any attention as I reverently handle the real stallion's shaft, the smooth skin behind the head calling my attention.

"Mmm… You like that, don't you?"
I shudder.
"Yes, sir, I love your big dick."
The words feel right and wrong coming from my lips at the same time, tail lashing the air, though all I feel is arousal, arousal to the extreme. I tenderly take the fat flare of his cock, thicker than mine already and he was not even fully engorged, between my lips, suckling and teasing, playing my tongue into the dip in the middle, though what I am really doing is seeking out every last sensitive spot that I can. I need to find everything, absolutely everything, to please him, to make him snort and stomp and whinny and blow a load, right in my muzzle.

But my lips cannot delve down over his cock just yet, oh no. No, there was sweeter delights to be savoured in the meaty length, too thick for me to encircle his prick with my finger and thumb. The bay stallion, whose name that I don't know, must be a draft breed of some kind, but I can't find it in myself to care as I nuzzle and lap down the smooth, taut length of his cock to the medial ring, marvelling at how many inches and laps that took me. I had thought that my cock was big enough, but, well… Who'd want a prick like mine when that tail hole destroying stud-fucker was around? No wonder I wasn't getting any tail.

His cock was better though: so, so much better… All I want to do is to stay there, down on my knees forever, tugging gently at the medial ring with my lips, where the skin past it moves more freely over his length. The wrinkles there smooth out as I caress and tease, the fat head pulsing and drooling, though I catch what I can in my paw, smearing it over the head and the first few inches of his dick…for later.

The sheath calls my attention as much as the rest of his cock, for I cannot leave one part of him out when I am there to savour and seduce the stud stallion with every fibre of my being. My tongue dips sweetly inside, tasting his musk, that thick, masculine scent of him that screams *stallion*. I may be a stallion but there is no way in the world that I will ever be a stallion like him, never in a million years.

I don't want to be either, for that would not allow me to kiss and lap my way back up his dick as he shudders above me, only to take his cock-tip into my maw. With a raunchy thrust of his hips, it pushes into the back of my throat and I grunt, my muzzle built for mouth-fucking. I am only there to suck cock, his cock, an object to be used and a hole to be filled. My tongue cradles the underside of his cock, but the weighty meat of him is too much for the fleshiness of that appendage to handle, even as I moan, letting the soft vibrations travel from my lips into his length. He shudders and I press on, slipping down, my nose kissing his sheath, though I can only draw back.

For in the love of his cock is my adoration of it too, allowing my lips to caress and massage every last inch of his sweetly delicious, divine, succulent length like never before. I suck him down hungrily into my throat, letting the bulge rest there, right at the back, though I thank my lack of a gag reflex, not for the first time, as he slips down a little deeper.

"Mmph… What a skilled little whore cock-sucker you are."

I shudder. Yes… Yes, that's what I am. That's all I need to be, reverently adoring horse dicks, day in and day out. I suckle him down, though I can still breathe, even as he pushes into my throat, holding my mane, fucking my mouth, fucking me as if my mouth is just a passing fancy to him, a hole to be filled.

I am only a hole to be filled. And I *fucking love it*.

There's nowhere else I'd rather be as I struggle to control and manage his thick length on my tongue, squeezing it up to the smooth, grey underside, though the pound of his medial ring pressing even deeper makes my heart sing. Oh, how I want it, even more, though I hardly had the chance to worship the stud's nuts too. That can be fixed, however, as he holds my head roughly in place by my mane, fucking my mouth, my paws finding his nuts and cradling them, teasing, massaging. There is nothing rough at all to be had in the touch of my paws and fingers around his balls, only reverence and worship, for even his balls massively surpass mine.

"Unff… Horny little slut…"

But he is horny too and I feel it in him, how the tenor of his hips increases, pace driving, the fleshy tip of his cock swelling as I moan around him. Yes, oh, yes, I need it, give it to your little suck-slut-stallion!

It pumps out, so fleshy and delicious, in my mouth and I manage one last squeeze of his nuts as he erupts on my tongue and down my throat, grunting and groaning, the very best that a stud stallion has to offer. It drools down my throat, though blast after blast cannot help but be sent right where it belongs, my throat working, gulping, striving with all my might simply to take him down. I need it all, not wanting to let a single drop go to waste, but he keeps thrusting and fucking my muzzle as if he cannot stop for the passion of it all, ramming past my lips and driving deep. Cum spurts and dribbles out of the corners of my lips as I howl, my cries muffled, around his dick, wanting it all, feeling every throbbing pulse those virile nuts have to offer me.

More and more… I feel it slide down my throat, so slick and thick and creamy. I never want to stop drinking it down, his thrusts slowing, the taste of his musk hanging in the air around me, the scent tickling at my nostrils. My own dick has not softened and is as hard as ever, though it is not me that takes that pleasure from orgasm but him, the stud, the dominant stallion. I am only lucky to be allowed to get down on my knees before him, whimpering, submitting, serving.

I couldn't imagine that I could ever want anything more as I kneel there, submitting to him, whimpering for him, the stud stallion towering over me. He doesn't have to do anything at all to be simply as dominant as he wants to be, snorting and heaving with great, big puffs of breath. If I roll my eyes back, I can just about take in the scope of his glorious abs, though a few more years and it will be a muscle-gut, the stallion older than me. But that is just why he has so much bulk and heft and size to him, a stud who can be proud of the name, while I am a growing slut-stallion, more of a colt than a stallion. I don't know if I'll ever be as good or as strong as him, not in any way.

But I get to enjoy his thick, slippery cream pouring down my throat, breathing shortly and sharply through my nostrils as he drags my head dominantly all the way down. There is not a millimetre more cock left that he could possibly jam into my mouth as I huff and pant around him, tongue flickering and caressing, though even my attempts there in that regard fall short and weak against his muscled might. Every pulse of cum shooting down the length of his filly-making fuck meat sends me trembling, knowing that there is no way that I could ever hope to match up to him, let alone to ever be his better.

That is my only place in life, even as he pulls back to hose down my face and neck with his cream, dripping and drooling, so much of it slopping down that I can barely take it. Cum drips down my face, pouring over my eyelids, and I can hardly believe that he is *still* cumming, my nostrils quivering even as his cum paints them.

"Open wide, slut…"

He hooks his finger into the corner of my lips just to make sure that I do open up obediently for him, but, by that point, I am completely and utterly lost to the will of the stallion like I've never done in my lifetime. I moan for him, shuddering in place, hips rocking, my cock hard, so very hard, yet no one has anything to do with that. I catch what cum I can in my mouth, swallowing greedily, gulping it all down, snorting and heaving, my chest juddering with every heady snatch of much-needed breath.

I want it. I crave it. Yet there is nothing I can do to get it. I am at his whim and his will, no more than that.

He bears me back with a heady snort and I find myself on his bed, the sheets rumpling under my back, though I don't care about the discomfort. My cock splays out across my belly, woefully on show, as his flared cock-tip presses to my most intimate region, the pucker tucked up under my tail.

It's all on show, everything exposed, my need rising, snorting, heaving, grunting. I need it even as the stud whose name I still don't know grinds into me, deeper and deeper. My hole is spreading open around him before my mind even knows it, though the crash of pleasure alerts me, waves of lust swamping my form.

"Unff…" He grunts, powering in, not caring for any strain as he takes his pleasure. "So tight… Not quite the whore you…grr…pretend to be."

I never thought I'd be on my back before him so swiftly, not when first meeting him, but my legs splay even more submissively for him, drinking in the sight of his form, all his muscles, the stud powering into me. He grunts and whinnies, smirking as he takes me, my legs hooked up and drawn further back towards my chest, all to allow him the best access possible. And it is me that feels every inch of his cock powering into my tight backside, slick with cum and saliva, though I would have taken him anyway. Where there is no choice, I rise to the occasion.

His snorts fill the room, but it is my dick that cannot help but rise. Thrust after thrust slams into my prostate, making me buck and whinny, though there is hardly any space for me to move into, mostly immobile in such a position. I grunt and he ignores it, though his ears twitching, mane spilling roughly down the brown arch of his neck, the need of him shuddering in powerful muscle. Sweat gleams on his body, dripping and soaking his coat, and I moan lustfully as I inhale it, greedily taking in the hot musk of him, all for my pleasure.

Every inch of his cock powers into me as if it is trying to make me intimately familiar with its divine right, grinding in harder and faster, deeper, my own shaft throbbing. My nuts ache and I let out an ear-splitting whinny in the heartbeat before orgasm takes me, balls overfilled, my body overstimulated, though there is nowhere else at all that I would rather be. My cock shoots my load over my stomach, a few shots reaching my chest, though my reach and volume are nowhere near as much as the stud ramming into me, taking me so brutally, so lustfully, so carnally.

I was never meant to match up to him. And that's okay too.

He doesn't stop, merely smirking as I unload, my dark length lying half-soft against my stomach, drooling, the viscousness of my cum making it cling to my black hide as if it is part of his prize in taking me. He needs me as he thrusts, my body a vessel for him, cum slick on my muzzle, still dripping, some drying where the layer is thinner.

Thrust.

I moan, wanting it, reaching for him when I cannot cling.

Thrust.

He slams in, hips bouncing off my glutes and the backs of my thighs, grunting with every stroke.

Thrust.

His body, so masculine, dipping the sunshine of the gods… I'd do anything to touch it, to adore it, to worship the beast of a stallion until the end of my days.

He slams in, harder and faster, so close to his high, yet his masculine snort rumbles over me as he climaxes once again. His jiggling, fat nuts bounce off my ass with every stroke of his fuck-stick, meat slamming in, as deep as possible, not allowing a single bit of his reverent girth to go to waste. Yet it is all sealed inside my ass as he climaxes with a full-throated whinny, deeper than mine, though I should have already expected that.

Ropes of cum splash up into my backside, though, dimly, some part of me tells me that I should not be able to feel that, not really. I should not be that sensitive yet, with him, I am, sensing his load, how it swells into me, pumped deeper and deeper by the driving length of his cock. It is as if he is trying to force it up inside me all the more, snorting and grunting, his body overpowering mine in the very best of ways.

My hole squeezes around him, even though I should be relaxing, reminding him of his might and power, the "studliness" of him. Maybe that's why he chose me, why, ultimately, I was the very best choice for him, ramming in, cramming every inch of his dick into my slutty hole. There'll never be any way to tell, not even as I find myself before the dominant stud, night after night, letting him fuck me into mindless moan after moan.

"Nice and loose now…" He rumbles. "But not done yet."

For he has more in store for me that I don't even know about, snorting and pushing, stretching out my ass just a little more for his dick, all for his pleasure. My eyes roll, head falling back, barely able to hold my legs up anymore. I nicker throatily.

For the love of horse cock…I will do it all again.

Riding the Gym Stud

The stallion was glorious in his natural form, though Grayson surely had spent a lot of time honing his physical form, considering the sheer amount of time that the paint stallion spent at the gym. It was not that he didn't want to be there or was doing it merely for physical fitness – it was just one of his safe spaces, where he felt like he belonged. The community of guys, whether they were bulkier and focused on building muscle like him or just starting out on their journey with different goals, made him feel welcomed there from the very first day. With a community like that, well, would Grayson really not have wanted to go back? He looked forward to the gym at the end of every workday – and often at the weekend too.

Regardless of what was going on in his life, he always found some time, however little there was, to prioritise himself and the space that made him feel as if everything was okay with himself and the world around him.

Sometimes, that was all a guy needed.

Or, sometimes…they needed a little something more.

Grayson's ears twitched, topless that day, for it was getting on into the evening and, honestly, he never liked bench pressing with a shirt on. Squats yes, just to have a tiny barrier between his skin, coat and the barbell resting across his back, but he just felt more comfortable shirtless when he was down on a bench. Equine anthros, much like the humans scurrying around their world and a few other mammalian furs, were some of few that sweated all over their bodies, not just from specific glands, so it was not always that easy to regulate his temperature.

Still, it attracted looks and his interest had been perked, especially as the donkey eyed him up from the others side of the rack room. He'd only slid the bench back into a half-rack, not feeling like a full one that caged him in that day, the barbell rising and falling as he kept his hips down on the bench, along with his shoulder blades. The arch of his chest, pushing up as if bowed, spoke of his form, the care that he gave to his workouts, muscles bulging and straining obviously as Grayson forced them to contract under the heavy weight.

"Oof…"

That wasn't him: that was the donkey. And he would have been a liar if he had said that he wasn't putting on a bit of a show for him. The gym was quiet enough that night and, well, there were more than a few there that would fall prey to showing off, in a sense, though no one would do anything dangerous to themselves. Grunting heavily, he forced the bar back up, straining through, chest aching, until he slotted it back into the rack with a heavy exhalation.

He liked being watched. Where it made others self-conscious, it made him feel better placed to do what he came there to do, rubbing a towel around the back of his neck and shoulders and shooting the grey donkey a grin. The donkey's ears juddered up straight and he whipped back around to one of the machines on the other side of the room, across from the open space that people used for lifting on the thick matting. Grayson snickered, need stirring between his legs.

"Why don't you come over here and spot me?" He nickered flirtatiously, bolder than he had been on first joining that particular gym. "I could use some company."

The donkey gulped visibly, though was quick enough to join him, not seeming to quite know what to do with his hands – but that was alright. Grayson could soon put them to use, if the donkey was up for it too.

"Heh, didn't mean to stare," the donkey said, extending a hand with hoofed fingertips, rough and blunt where they had been neatly filed, to the stallion. "Wish I could lift like that, though I know it takes time. I'm Lewis, by the way."

Grayson grinned.

"Grayson. And I'll help you, if you like. We're all, you know, doing our best for one another around here. Or I'd say talk to Jordan, one of the trainers – I always got on very well with him, knows his stuff."

The donkey settled, a little more at ease, though Grayson would have been a fool not to catch the coy grin tugging at his lips. It was not as if Lewis was trying all that hard to hide it.

"Can I spot you?"

Grayson didn't need a spot, but he nodded anyway. He was done with his workout for the night, having worked in some of his smaller exercises throughout his chest routine on the bench. But that did not mean at all that he was not eager to see where things went.

Foreplay. That was the best way to put it as he looked up between Lewis' strong legs, the donkey wearing shorts, like him, though the bulge there was more impressive than the muscle that he had already built. It was all Grayson could do to concentrate as he looked up practically between the donkey's legs, the jack standing too close to him for comfort. But it was never meant to be comfortable as he shifted into position, setting his hands on the bar, and grunted through his reps.

His chest ached, shoulders trying to take the strain as he compensated, though Grayson only found it laughable that he was still trying to concentrate on lifting. For who could really concentrate, after all, with the musk of a donkey like Lewis swelling to fill the air, the intrinsic scent of a male in need, his sheath obviously showing through while his cock grew? He did not expect himself to hold back for so long, the jack's tail swinging with need, but Grayson enjoyed the moment, the rush of pleasure as he did another bench press rep.

"Unff!"

The bar sank towards his chest, brushing it, before rising again, muscles contracting to complete the rep. And yet Grayson's cock too rose to attention as if it had merely been waiting for the opportune moment to make itself known, to show the donkey exactly what effect he had on him. Perhaps it was a bit quick to be turned on by the donkey's junk practically hanging in his face, but, really, it had been the jack's eyes on him that had done the trick for him, well and truly. The lure of being watched was just something Grayson could not resist, the stallion grunting, trying and failing to concentrate on his lift.

Yet he could not help but smirk as his cock ached and throbbed, plumping up as it filled with blood and pushed from his sheath, swelling into his shorts. He hadn't put on any underwear for that session, thinking he could be discreet enough at that hour, but it was not as if something was holding him back there, stopping him from showing off his need while Lewis did the same. Maybe it was fate to show off his assets in such an open manner, the donkey juddering behind him.

Grayson smirked. That must have meant that Lewis had spotted his dick too.

"Unff… Well, you don't seem to mind the attention."

The donkey laughed a little nervously, though seemed to pull on some store of confidence as the stallion re-racked the barbell with a grunt, chest heaving. He collapsed back to the bench, sweat slickening his back lightly where he laid down along the bench, his nose twitching and eyes half-lidded as he followed the path of the donkey around before him. The swing in his steps dragged the horse's eyes down to his cock and butt, the thick round of it, though Grayson by no means minded having a little extra to grab on to down there.

"Fuck," he hissed out through his teeth, though the word was softened in a nicker, snorting and grunting throatily. "You could have just asked me to go back to the changing rooms, you know…"

The donkey grinned, turning his back to Grayson as he toyed with the hem of his shorts.

"Yeah… But where would the fun be in that?"

Grayson privately thought, honestly, there would have been rather a lot of fun in that too, but the words slipped from his lips as Lewis bent over, tugging his shorts down. His underwear came along with his exterior clothing, revealing a thick rump with muscle beneath a pleasing layer of fat, the kind of butt that the stallion could absolutely imagine bending over some of the equipment and going to town on. He grunted, cock throbbing, a damp spot showing through his shorts as he lay there, waiting on the jack, in a position of power with his rippling muscles. Suddenly, the aches and gentle strains of his workout no longer seemed all that important, re-energised with a smirk tugging at his lips.

The donkey stripped off his shirt too, dragging it over his head, and Grayson freed his erection, shoving his shorts down just enough to let the hot length out of its temporary prison. The stifled bray of the jack made his heart pound even more, hands lifting to the barbell as if the stallion needed something to support him, though he was quite comfortable where he was. It was flattering too how the donkey's eyes locked on to the rising swell of his cock, a good third bigger and thicker than Lewis', though it was not a competition. Not in the name of pleasure and lust, all so deliciously and deliriously tangled together, like they were always meant to be.

"You sure you can take that?" Grayson grunted, eyes dancing with wicked glee. "It gets bigger too…"

Lewis licked his lips, his long donkey ears twitching.

"Yeah, I bet," he groaned throatily, boldly taking the horse's cock in his hand. "You not worried about getting caught then?"

Grayson grinned.

"Mm… I could be more worried."

He knew that things could get a bit rough, to be fair, if they were caught, but that notion was swept away from his mind in any capacity as the donkey's lips folded teasingly around the tip of his cock. The soft flexibility of them tugged and pulled at his soft flare, though it could easily bloom with the right stimulation, the fleshy, spongy head aching for every bit of stimulation Lewis was willing to give him. Grayson grunted, rocking his hips up to meet the jack, though he otherwise allowed him to do exactly what he wanted, to take shared pleasure just as they pleased.

There didn't have to be any rush to it either, not even as the musk of equines filled the air, his nostrils puckering and flaring, dragging in heady breath after breath. His hands tightened on the barbell and his smug smirk deepened, as if keeping it off his face was beyond the realm of any possibility. He grunted, rolling his hips up, the donkey opening his mouth wide to take him inside, cradling his thick length on his tongue.

Even for an anthro without a gag reflex, the donkey struggled to take his length down his throat, though Lewis did not seem put off at all by Grayson's size. His hand closed around the rest of the horse's dick to pump and stroke what he could not gulp down, straining as if he was trying to keep his eyes open but was not quite able to. It was a beautiful thing to watch someone come apart so completely as they sucked his cock, the air of exhibitionism, of doing it all in a place where he felt so very comfortable and yet exposed, trembling through the stallion.

It was hot... So much so that he didn't honestly know why he hadn't tried it before. There had been looks before, yes, flirting before, yes – but never directed at him. There had been a scent of males in need before too, at the gym, but he'd never dug into it, even if that day had turned out to be exactly everything he'd needed and more.

"Unff... Fuck yes... God, that feels good..."

"Wait until you feel this," Lewis said, drawing back with a slurp and smack of his lips, pre-cum strung out between the head of Grayson's cock and his lips. "Just...hang tight..."

He turned, giving the stallion the best view of his rump once more, swinging a leg over him and the bench to straddle him. Grayson would have warned him about the lack of lube, but the donkey seemed determined, one way or the other, groaning deep in the back of his throat as the thick flare sprung up against his tail hole.

"Fuck..."

"Mmmph, yeah, take it slow..."

Grayson didn't want to hurt him, after all, not as the donkey sank, his thick, brown doughnut of flesh stretching lightly, more and more, around the stallion's dick. He went slowly, though pleasure swamped the stallion, hardly able to believe what he was doing in practically public, nickering throatily as his tail tried to swish from where it was trapped between his bare buttocks and the bench.

Yet it was perfect exactly as it was, hot and sweaty, relishing in the carnal moment. Grayson helped the donkey out by holding his cock up for him, so that he didn't have to reach back to keep it in position while his body took care of the rest, but the jack didn't seem to need much help either. The equine's large hands landed on his backside, groping and squeezing, fingers folding in around his hips as he swallowed a deep groan, wondering just how far they would get without being discovered.

There were cameras in there, after all… The real question was, with what Grayson already suspected was apt to go on in that gym, if anyone would bother coming to tell them to cut it out or even anything more than that.

With all that had been said, Grayson had already rolled the dice, the donkey's ass sinking on to his cock, squeezing devoutly, as if there was no other world outside them and the gym, not right then. All that mattered was just how hard Lewis could lustfully squeeze around his cock, as if the jack was trying to increase his stimulation even more, though the clench and pull of such muscles was erratic at best. There was only so much either of them could do, after all, Grayson finally stilling the donkey once he had sunk past the medial ring.

It was about time he took Lewis for a ride, after all…

The donkey's groans echoed through the gym, as much as he tried to quiet himself, thrust after thrust of the stallion powering up into his backside. He grunted and heaved, whimpering for more, though Grayson was prepared to give him all that he desired and more. The suck and light slickness of the jack's tail hole tugging around him was too exquisite to pass up as he snorted heavily, nostrils fluttering, thrusting and grinding with raw abandon.

"Unff… Fuck, you're tight…"

Lewis didn't have any words for that, his cock bobbing in the air before him, drooling a slick spill of pre-cum. He didn't look at all as if he was far off cumming and, for once, time may well have been of the essence. Planting his hooves more firmly, Grayson grunting, thrusting with all the power he had in his lower half, muscles bulging, slamming up into the jack to a screech of a bray.

He should have been quieter, yes, but they just couldn't help themselves as they took what was their due, two studly bodies, each in their way, finding all that they needed in one another. The tightness of the jack's backside goaded Grayson on, though the jack pumped his cock too with one hand, making sure that other nuances of his pleasure did not go untended too, even where the stallion could not quite reach. Grunting and thrusting, arousal aching through him, burning under his skin, the stallion dimly thought that he could give the jack another go around if only he came back to his place later that night.

Or another time. Any time, really, would be good, when it was the same thing they both wanted.

They groaned, not caring if they were caught, trapped in carnal lust, pre-cum slickening the way for Grayson's cock. Only when Lewis opened up and softened around him did he thrust harder and harder, grinding in forcibly, spurred on by the donkey's grunts and half-muffled brays. He must have had his hand clapped over his snout, trying to quiet himself, but he wasn't doing a very good job of it at all.

Grayson rather liked that.

The donkey's cock drooled slickly, though Grayson bit his lip, flare thickening and plumping up within Lewis' deliciously tight backside. He groaned, trying to hold back for as long as possible, but, in the end, it was the donkey that spilt over the edge, tumbling in a freefall of desire. He let out his loudest bray yet, echoing through more of the industrial unit gym, bouncing off the walls and surely alerting adjoining units too as to what was going on in there. But no one cared, no one came to find them, not as Lewis painted the grey flooring with his seed, the paint stallion driving up into his pucker until he too found release.

And that was how they met, though not the story that they would later tell to friends and family. Not about Grayson filling his donkey lover with so much cream that it spilt over, drooling out from the join of their bodies and slopping over his crotch, slickening his sheath, making a further mess of the bench and floor. Not about how the donkey had had to run out to his car afterwards, still dripping and drooling, his cock shoved down the leg of one of his shorts. And certainly not about how they fucked in the back of the car in the car park again for a second time after that, unable to get enough of each other.

It was one hell of a story and it was their story, neither stallion nor jack wanting to change a thing.

Riding a gym stud, after all, could *never* have bad consequences…

Sunset at the Beach

"Hey, how're you doing?"

With their surfboards lying on the sand beside their sun loungers, the anthro equine and the man with a hint of afternoon stubble around his chin were a regular sight on the beach – at least, in the summer months. Families had gone home for the day as the availability of surfing on the beach petered out with the lifeguards retiring, the beach closed at the eve of the day. Of course, they had stayed, hiding around the back of the rocks until everyone else had been cleared out, waves crashing down on the Cornish coastline sending seafoam up the sand even as the tide went out.

They were a pair indeed, the stallion a good head and shoulders, as an anthro, taller than his human partner, Kade. Kade was roughly five foot eight with a rough "surfer" tousle of blonde hair that was more sun-kissed than ever that year. With the sunset touching the sea, his boyfriend was even hotter, to him, than ever before, the crimson and orange of the sunset brushing his chestnut coat, setting off the red hues in the hairs.

Neither were particularly thickly muscled, but that was not the point of it, their bodies on the leaner side, toned and functionally fit. Regular work and day jobs were all well and good for the two of them, but the long, hot summer months were all that the two of them lived for as they relaxed there, taking a moment of peace while their muscles ached from surfing all day – or at least a good portion of it. Some of the time had been spent getting more pizza than they were proud to admit from the shack at the beach.

Damn, if it wasn't so good…

Vicente grunted, the stallion stretching out, his glasses balanced on his nose, though they were not the easiest shades for an equine anthro to wear. The ones that were custom-made for him clipped into his mane behind his ears, which he preferred over the ones that actually hooked behind his ears. He didn't want to offend anyone, but the stallion thought they looked kind of geeky.

"Hey, are you listening to me?"

Kade grinned, pushing his shades down his nose, blue eyes dancing with mischief over the top. All alone there… Well, they had their sunshade, the windbreaker, set up to block them partially from view, but they were not, in particular, trying to hide the fact that they were down there on the beach. No one cared, not when they were locals and regulars anyway, and to get away with a few more things, well…

…Kade had been looking for something a little flirtier for some time.

The first Vicente knew of his partner getting a little more up close and personal with him was Kade swinging his leg over the horse's midsection and sitting on his abs. Vicente grunted softly, shaking his head, though Kade was not about to be put off so easily. He arched his back, showing off his topless upper half with ease, the rich tan of his skin denoting his mixed heritage and more than a fair amount of time spent in the sunshine that year already. Bringing the best of the Mediterranean to the Cornish coastline, he could barely believe his luck in finding such a sexy stallion to spend the rest of his days with.

That was if Vicente would have him. But he could only hope and try, looking to the future.

"What do you think you're doing?"

Vicente snorted and eyed up his boyfriend, but, truly, he already knew what was going on, even if he was in the business of playing the big, bad stud horse who was far too "cool" for that sort of thing. His sheath tingled at the thought of it, tail flicking under his buttocks, though the velvety dock was pinned down in such a position where it would not become trapped or crushed.

"Come on…"

Kade smirked, tossing his shades aside, the cut of his jaw smoothly chiselled, though an old acne scar on his forehead reminded the equine anthro that, despite his jaw-dropping good looks, his boyfriend was, in fact, still human. Which was just as well, as he did sometimes chance to act as if he was a god who had been sent down to the land to be worshipped, getting what he wanted with a coy smile and a hand placed carefully where it belonged on his boyfriend's body.

The horse's shaft pulsed, easing out a fraction more from his sheath. He couldn't have said whether Kade noticed or not, even if that was clearly his intent, waves washing up on the shore, rushing and pulling with the flow of the tide.

"Come on, no one's looking…"

There was no one there, that was true, but Vicente still raised an eyebrow as Kade got his cock out in one hand, the rod of flesh thickening up swiftly in the clutch of his fingers. Although it was not as thick as what Vicente was boasting, tucked away in his swim trunks, best suited to chilling out at the beach, it was a good size for a man, more than enough to handle. The stallion snorted softly, rumbling a throaty chuckle, but hardly had a chance to bring his hand up in time to do anything about it before Kade shuffled up his body.

One thing about equine anatomy was that the crest of the neck and the way that the vertebrae aligned in the neck meant that it was possible for him to tip his chin down to his chest too, even if it was not comfortable. It was not a position that Vicente would have been comfortable holding for any length of time, but he was keener than he perhaps should have been as Kade pushed his shaft, insistently, up against his lips.

"A little kiss, you know you want to…"

Oh, he was cheeky and suave and thought he was the gift of the gods to earth and more – at least, that was how Vicente thought the saying went – but he was Vicente's and the stallion was not about to let him go, not in any day and age. Neither was he about to let the treat of his boyfriend's cock go to waste, lustfully shivering at the thought of doing it out there, in the open. Sure, the beach was deserted and twilight was rapidly descending as sunset touched the sea and sand, fading, bringing them into a softer wrap of evening entirely.

That cock slipped into his mouth as if it was meant to be there, pushing in, his muzzle easily big enough to take it. Even though Vicente had more typically delicate features, including a smooth dish to his cheek, the stallion was still stronger and larger, even if he could allow his strength and size to be set aside for Kade's pleasure.

Kade groaned, head falling back, his hand on the back of Vicente's head, though he did not need to guide the horse anthro down on his cock as the stud slurped down his shaft expertly. He knew what his boyfriend loved and gave it all to him in spades, moaning around his shaft just to give him a little more sensation. The skin of Kade's uncut length pushed back and moved over his shaft as Vicente's head bobbed, ears twitching and flicking, the stallion losing himself in a moment that he had not even been aware was coming to him that day.

The cool of the late evening wind tickling his hide was all well and good, though they could not be out there for much longer in the fold of twilight, gulls settling down to roost on the cliffs not far away for the night. Vicente's cock thickened up, forming a huge bulge in his trunks, though they could not be pulled down so easily, not with Kade in the way, blocking him there. Vicente grunted, hips juddering, yet that extra sensation had him shuddering like nothing ever had before, hooves on either side of the lounger, digging into the sand.

His bare hooves left scuffed up prints in the soft sand as he bore down, though there was a little more moisture in it than there had been first thing that morning. He squirmed, not feeling like so much of a stud stallion as Kade fucked his muzzle, humping slowly, making good use of every inch of stallion muzzle that he had there to take. It was strange to give oral like that, to feel like he was on the bottom well and truly when they usually passed control back and forth between the two of them, all kinds and all positions. But with nothing between them being off-limits, that meant that they were open, more so than ever, to explore more and more.

Kade thrust and groaned, not quiet at all, though he knew that Vicente was hornier than ever as his cock swelled, reaching back, though it was difficult for him to balance on top of the stallion and grasp his cock at the same time. That did not stop him from trying, of course, lust getting the better of him, sweaty and off-balance and laughing giddily as he got his cock sucked. He rather liked the risk, the thought of discovery, even if it may not have been at all as kinky if it had actually happened, no.

His cock throbbed, spilling tiny drops of pre-cum. He'd never really formed anything that noticeable before getting with Kade, but perhaps it was something in the horse that had drawn it out of him. He could not say, Kade gasping, squeezing the stallion's cock through his trunks, lusting for the moment there exactly as it was. There was nothing, nothing at all, that could have made it more perfect than it already was, a cock pushing into his boyfriend's mouth, his need rising.

But Kade was not a stallion and to hold anything back would have been impossible for him, even as he grunted and moaned, rolling his head back.

"Ohhh, oh, fuck…"

Too much, too hot, that thick length of fleshy stallion tongue squeezing up to the underside. Even while Kade's dick was within his muzzle, the horse lapped and lapped, suckling on it, his cheeks trying to hollow, though it was in a different place than ever the hollowing would have been seen on a human. His lips themselves might have been small, but Vicente more than knew how to use them, succulently squeezing and teasing, applying differing levels of pressure, all to see Kade shudder so deliciously before him.

It was all he needed, all that he could ever have craved, moaning out loud, thrusting, rocking his hips up, losing sense of himself in a moment where all that mattered was just how he and Kade came together. Vicente sucked his partner into his mouth, his hands on Kade's hips, his buttocks, squeezing, driving and encouraging him, on, for he needed it even more, still so very much more.

"Oh…"

But Kade could not hold back as Vicente forced him over the edge, expertly swirling his tongue around his cock, drawing out more and more from him, whimpering and groaning, though neither of them could any longer see any reason to keep it down or quiet at all. If anyone was going to walk in on them, they would have already done so – at least, that was what they chose to believe.

He thrust and thrust, clinging to the horse's ears, grunting, gasping, fingers twisted into his mane.

Vicente could not have drawn back even if he'd wanted to, so it was just as well that every fibre of the horse's being wanted him to thrust on, taking spurts of seed into his mouth. Although the man's cock was smaller than what he was boasting, hardly tucked away in his swim trunks, it was the perfect fit for him, swallowing down dollops of seed that would have worked their way down his throat one way or the other anyway otherwise.

The stallion grunted, soft lips folded around that cock until Kade could take it no more, softening and drawing back with a laugh, the wrap of twilight holding them softly yet firmly in its arms.

"Oof… Vicente, it's getting late. We should really… Ahhh…"

The stallion's tongue flickered out tenaciously, stroking down the man's too sensitive cock-tip. He shuddered and drew back, but the horse himself was yet to be pleased, wrapping his arms around Kade as he got his hooves under him properly, digging into the sand. Kade squeaked as Vicente hefted him up in his arms, standing with only a little difficulty, the man squirming, wriggling, though he did not want to be let down, not at all.

No, all he needed was to be tossed down on to the sand, Vicente moving over him, overpowering him fully even as Kade cried out for it.

"Ah, yes… Fuck… God, Vicente, what are you doing to me?"

For it was hard to phrase the delicious lust coursing through him in any other manner, his cock trying to harden up all over again, even though it was too soon for him to get off again. His body was there, however, for Vicente's pleasure, the stallion pinning him down, on all fours, the stud's cock finally out and hard, in all its glory. It was so thick around that Kade could not close his fingers around it, though he knew, even then, it would be more difficult than usual for him to take the entire length of the stallion's shaft into his backside without lube.

It would be fine though, as long as Vicente was gentle with him. And he knew that his lover would be, his partner, his boyfriend… Whatever the hell it was that they all wanted to call each other. It was up to them, but it was in that moment more than any other that he belonged to the stud stallion, the only one who had ever made him want to change, to be a better man.

Maybe that's what true love was. Maybe it was stolen kisses and salt on lips, fucking on a beach when there was no one there to stop them, to bear witness to the illicit nature of their tryst. Kade grunted, stifling his groans as much as he could as Vicente took him, squeezing in thick inch after inch of his stud-stick, his prick demanding more. It was only more that Kade had to give him too, struggling to brace on his hands and arms, rocking back, rolling his hips with shuddering lust, wanting more.

But Vicente knew his boyfriend, what he could take, taking his time even as sweat layered his coat, a light sheen of froth around his lips, at the corners, where he had been licking and chewing with lust. His heavy nuts throbbed and ached to spill his load, but he held off, if only for his own pleasure. Kade could have taken his seed at any time, any time at all, but Vicente wanted to feel more, thrusting and grinding, pushing deep, easing in past the medial ring as Kade gasped and groaned.

In the cool grasp of twilight, the sea washing ever closer on the shore as the tide came in, Kade ground back against Vicente, though the stallion was in control in that moment. He gripped Kade's shoulder lustfully, curling his fingers around, holding him in place, each drive of his hips coming with an ever-increasing degree of savageness. It was all wanted, of course, all needed, yet Kade gasped and groaned, deeply and gutturally, as if he could not take it at all, arching back, head swimming, lust spinning and turning him around and around.

It almost felt as if he was not present in the moment at all with so much emotion washing over him, everything all at once, grunting thickly, his ass so full, so very stretched, with that thick length of stallion dick. Vicente thrust harder and harder, demanding that he opened up around him, Kade's body trembling, aching for it all, needing it so very much more than Vicente could have ever anticipated. Yet the man's lust was best placed where he would always be in the arms of his lover, waves crashing on the shore, a gull calling out nearby, perhaps shuffling its wings as they settled more comfortably into where they had chosen to roost.

Vicente snorted heavily, lost in the moment, thrusting, grinding, the smack of his hips on Kade's backside rising more than their groans. However the man was able to take his full length, he'd never know – but he did not have to know when everything felt so good, exactly as he was. He pounded Kade as if they would never again get the chance to fuck, even though that very much was not true, the man's ass tight around him as he thrust and thrust.

Yet there was nothing else at all that mattered for them, not even the threat of getting caught, except each other. The tightness of Kade's ass squeezing around Vicente's cock had the stallion hunching over him, feral and raw in the heat of the moment, driving in harder and faster, needing it all, every last second of it. The medial ring tugged at his partner's backside with every thrust of his cock, pounding and slamming,

Kade's breath catching, though his partner was caught up in the heat of it all.

Cool air licked at their bodies as their passion rose and rose, Vicente's hand half-closing around his partner's shaft as it hardened up all over again. He needed it, though he was still getting hard, too sensitive and craving it, Vicente's strong, muscled body egging him on. Moments swirled into one another as the stallion pressed down over his back, sweat marking his hide, tail swishing, lashing the air in a release of tension. He had to cum though, thrusting harder and harder, snorting heavily, his chest heaving for every breath he snatched into his lungs.

Closer and closer…until he could not hold any of it back for a single moment more. All for him, letting out a bellowing roar of orgasm that was more dragon-like than stallion-like, though there was no one there that cared, not one bit. Vicente didn't stop thrusting, not even as his balls ached, driving in, deeper and deeper, as deep as he could possibly go while spurt after spurt of creamy seed filled his partner.

And all Kade could do was take it, thrust after thrust, stroke after stroke, spurt after spurt. It was needed, for the two of them, that moment that was spent between the two of them, only them, crying out, howling, twisting and grinding, their bodies all that mattered in the rhythm and the life of the world and ocean all around.

What they had not noticed, however, even as Vicente whuffled softly at the back of Kade's neck, trembling against him, the sea washing in always closer. It lapped at the end of the sun lounger that was a little closer to the water's edge and the horse snorted a chuckle, though he would not have been able to move, not yet, even if his cock was not rammed into his partner's backside, seated there comfortably. He barely rocked back and forth, staying as deep as it was possible for his cock to rest, the head flared and throbbing, his body striving to send every spurt of cum as deep as possible.

It was not needed…and yet it was lusted for, all the same, in delirious delight.

"Heh, hehe… We should probably…unff…move…"

Vicente was not convincing as Kade lowered his head, rocking back against him, as much as his legs trembled. The stallion let more and more of his weight bear down over the man's back, forcing him down, though there was little space for his more submissive partner to move into.

"Yeah… Hah… Maybe…"

But Kade was happy where he was, heart filling with lust and love, his cock mostly hard, the pressure up against his prostate too much to ignore. There was nowhere else in the world he would have preferred to be with that hot length of horse cock sealing every drop of cum inside him, lips parted in a breathy smile.

To be with Vicente was the greatest pleasure of all. And, despite the work they would have left to do that summer, making a living, he couldn't wait to see what more could come for them. Whether in sunset, in dawn, in day or in night: they would always find themselves together.

Between anthro stallion and man, there was nothing that either of them could want for.

Though maybe a few more kinky fucks on the beach could *very much* be in order!

Behind the Barn

"Unff… Oh, fuck… Quinn… You can't do that out here!"

The black and white stallion blushed heavily and tried to squirm away from his partner – but the other horse was not about to give up so easily. Around the side of the stables, halfway to the muck heap, Grady had been forced to drop the wheelbarrow down with a clank when Quinn had sensually folded his body around him. Grady still didn't know quite how Quinn managed to do that, for the stallion was moderately bulky from work around the yard and doing most of the manual labour there, though he somehow did it anyway.

Grady whined, nostrils fluttering, as a high-pitched squeal threatened to break free from him. But they could not be heard – they weren't exactly a known thing around the yard, or even further afield yet. And he had thought that he was okay with that, still coming to terms with his sexuality and all that his likes meant for him, although…it was more complicated than simply running through a few little words in his head. It was always going to be more complicated than that.

"Come on…" Quinn murmured, those skilful stallion lips teasing and lipping at his neck. "I just want to spend some time with you. You can say no, but I know you want to."

It was hard for Grady to deny that, more heat racing to his cheeks, though his shy embarrassment showed more in how his ears were flicking back and forth, twitching and turning. He was trying to stay on alert, even as the normal sounds of the stable yard layered the air, only the two of them over on that side of the yard. For two stallions who still had one hoof in the closet, it was something, at least.

And maybe they needed that something. Maybe that was just why Grady allowed the big, palomino stallion with feather around his bare fetlocks to draw him gently behind the old barn, the barn that creaked something dreadful when the weather was raging. They didn't know for how long it would stand but it held perfectly for Grady with his back against it and the glorious, beautiful glow of the palomino right there before him.

Quinn would never fail to take his breath away, he was sure, no matter how long they were together. There was just something about the stallion, something big, that made him want to know more, something that had raised his curiosity about Quinn all those months ago, back when he had just been questioning his sexuality. He'd had fun with mares, yes, and other anthros too, though he'd always had an eye for other body types – body types that were more often seen on male anthros. He'd tried getting with a cool bodybuilder mare who had hit all the right notes for him, though, unfortunately, the sizzling chemistry they had both longed for simply had not been there. They were still good friends and she was one of few who knew about him being with Quinn.

He just wasn't ready to be "out out" yet, even if that felt like it was a very silly thing to say when Quinn was folding to his knees, not seeming to drop much height at all, before him. The white spill of his mane cascaded down his neck as if he had been snatched off the cover of a romance novel and was just getting set up for his next shot. Not that Grady had ever said that to him, of course, except that time he had been drunk and confessed just how hot Quinn was. That was one time where the lowering of his inhibitions had benefitted him, as it had opened the door to something more between him and Quinn.

Something that was defined as exclusive and would be soon ready to go to the next level on, though there was no real rush. Not when Quinn was quietly confident in his sexuality, preferring to keep things quiet and maintaining that it was no one else's business what he liked. Yet he was like that with his geeky hobbies too, keeping them away from the stable yard and smiling and walking off if anyone found out and dare to tease him about them. To say that the stallion was unflappable in public was an understatement, yet Grady was learning just how much seemingly small things like that could get under the horse's skin.

He wanted to make things better, those little things and the big things too, for Quinn, where he could. And, soon, he would be ready for others to know about them too, even if it would take him a long time to really find himself and where he fit into the LGBTQ world.

There was time. There was no rush.

Well, there might have been a small amount of rush there with Quinn as the golden stallion smirked and nuzzled at his crotch, playfully lipping at his jodhpurs, which were tenting out with the swell of his cock. It pushed obviously from his sheath as Grady nickered throatily and bobbed his head, his tail not knowing whether to lash back and forth or clamp down. Either option revealed some measure of tension in him, although the stallion did not think that it was all that easy to release.

Better to allow Quinn to take care of that for him then.

"Mmm, you look so pretty like this," Quinn murmured, nuzzling again into his crotch and bumping the growing bulge. "Can I? No one's around, you can keep lookout…"

"I… Mmph…"

Grady nodded, winding his fingers into the stallion's hair, for he didn't quite trust himself to speak, not in that moment. He wanted it, yes, yet he had to place his trust in Quinn also, trusting the equine to keep both of them safe and in a good position. Getting caught and outed with his cock in someone else's mouth was, well…hot but not at all the way he wanted to come out.

"Heh… You just tell me if you need anything else, pony," Quinn nickered. "I got you."

He knew that. But it was still nice to hear it, huffing hotly through his flared nostrils and leaning back against the wood of the barn. It creaked a little from his weight, but everything was good, all as it meant to be, even as Quinn helped him get his cock out from his jodhpurs, unzipping them and fussing with the catch at the top. His balls were left inside while his sheath and shaft were freed, his cock blooming with blood as it thickened up with a soft flare at the head. Of course, it was not fully flared yet, as that would come at the point of orgasm. Yet it felt as if he was getting closer and closer to that already, prickles of tingling excitement clawing at his skin and nipping at his fetlocks.

His cock was mostly pink, which was not unusual, though there were a few mottled grey patches down near the base of it. They couldn't often be seen, not unless his sheath was peeled back, the span of his cock just after the medial ring, on the side closest to the head, a little thinner. The base was nice and thick and meaty though and the flare tended to grow dramatically at the point of orgasm, pulsing and throbbing when he sent spurt after spurt of thick cum out. All under the sweet and lusty will of Quinn's direction, of course. Quinn always knew how to get him off and how to edge him just a little so that his orgasm would be even stronger without frustrating him. It was one of the many, many things Grady was, slowly, falling in love with about Quinn. And maybe the stallion himself too.

"Such a beautiful cock…" Quinn grunted, a bulge in the stallion's jeans showing through, though Grady was not in a position to tend to it in any way. "Don't worry, Grady, I'm going to make you feel real good. Keep your ear out now, just in case. But you might kind of like that…"

Grady nipped at his lip, though was not quite able to catch it between his teeth. That was not too bad, yet Quinn's words gnawed at him, the stallion caressing his cock lightly with his hand, experimentally testing just how ready he was, how sensitive he was. Grady grunted and, emboldened, the stallion closed his hand around the base of Grady's cock, above the sheath, slowly pumping the last throbs of his cock all the way up to full, aching hardness.

Maybe he did like being out there, in the open air, not quite knowing if they were going to be walked in on, having the excitement of the risk. Yet it probably wouldn't be all that exciting if they really did get caught; until then, it was hot. Kind of. Maybe he'd work it out more later.

"Unff… Oh…"

Quinn's skilled lips pressed around the head of his cock, his hand still working up and down the length, pleasing and teasing, knowing exactly what he needed to do in order to get Grady's heart pounding. Grady shifted his weight, bright sunshine slanting across him, though it was not too warm yet, still only at the start of summer. He would think differently about the sunshine when the summer heat really hit them, but they'd have more than enough work in looking after, and riding too, the horses at the yard when the temperature escalated.

The golden stallion didn't seem to be paying attention, however, to how Grady shifted his weight, hooves digging in a little more to the patch of bare dirt. No, he was only focused on the treat of the stallion's cock right there before him, suckling tenderly on the head, letting his tongue swirl and pull around the sensitive glands. Grady grunted and thrust shortly, bucking his hips, though pulled back as if he was afraid of pushing too far, even if there was no possible way he could ever be too eager.

Not with Quinn. It would take even more time together, intimate time, for them to get to know one another, however. And that was okay too, for that was part of the beauty in getting to be with someone.

Not just in getting his cock sucked by a hot stud who was proving to be kinkier and kinkier, wanting to do more and more with him. And Grady was more than okay with that as he ran his fingers through the silken strands of Quinn's mane, tugging playfully on his forelock, even if he couldn't distract himself from the sensations overwhelming him, not then. He moaned openly, tongue flickering out against his lips and sweeping back, swallowing hard.

"Mmmph…"

"Mmm, a bit quieter, darling…"

Grady nodded. Yeah, he'd try. But Quinn's mouth was just so damn sensual as he grunted around his cock and dragged his mouth down the length, so slowly it was as if there was a lot more friction there than there actually was. Grady's heart pounded harder and faster and he felt himself breaking out into a light sweat, his body too warm under his clothes and yet not daring to disrobe further. The stallion's tongue cradled the underside of his cock as if it was meant to be there. For one thing that had surprised them both was just how well they fit together.

It was easy… Okay, they had had few arguments and spats and tension around each other's habits, though they were friends before they were partners and that definitely helped them both. Things could be okay, just like that, when they knew each other in a more intimate way and they were glad of it. Even more so as Quinn bobbed his head on Grady's cock, his nose going up and down, nostrils puckering and flaring as he took the head of the piebald stallion's cock into the back of his throat.

"Unff…"

Grady scuffled and scraped, the long length of his black tail twitching fervently back and forth, not able to stop himself. That was good, too good, sending a red-hot spike of pleasure through him, his abs and glutes contracting. The pressure of the stallion's throat around his cock made him want to thrust and grind, to hump like a stallion in "rut" – despite him knowing that rutting was more of a stag thing, but, to hell with it, he'd been around enough stags he felt he could use the word too. It was not breeding, no, not with a guy, but he wanted to spend himself, eyes a little wider and a little wilder, licking his lips and chewing at the air.

"Mmmmph!"

Quinn bobbed his head more and more quickly, squeezing the sheath right at the base, Grady rolling his hips forward without even thinking about it to get just a bit more stimulation on his balls. All it took was a little pressure, that was what he liked, and the hand at the base of his cock ground into them softly, just how he enjoyed it. The stallion did not back off that time, allowing Quinn to hump a little, setting the pace as his breathing came more and more quickly, raking through his chest, eyes half-closed, though there was a white edge to them as need sank its claws into him.

"Mmmph… Gonna…"

He swallowed the whinny that threatened to come as Quinn pulled his teeth, ever so lightly, over his swelling flare at just the right moment. That coupled with his muzzle, so long and perfect for kissing and sucking cock, was more than enough to send Grady stumbling unexpectedly over the edge, caught up in frenzied lust and swallowing every cry, otherwise, he would have been more than eager to let break free of his lips.

It was strange to have to be so quiet, yet exhilarating too. He heaved and panted, knowing that there was some measure of quiet to be had there, eyes half-closed, no longer even checking if there was anyone around them he should have been looking out for. Grady didn't even care, couldn't care, not as ecstasy flowed through him, tension in his loins as they ached and ached and sent great, pulsing spurts of cream straight down Quinn's eagerly waiting throat. The stallion gulped and swallowed like a pro, though he, to be fair, had had a bit more experiencing in sucking dicks than Grady had, even if he was swiftly catching up with the somewhat more experienced stallion. Yet it all showed in how Quinn massaged Grady's cock with his tongue (there was no other way for him to describe it), letting his saliva act as the lubricant as he lapped up against the underside to the extent he was able. Still bobbing his head softly, he kept at least two-thirds of Grady's cock inside his mouth at all times as the stallion spent every drop that his already sore balls had to give straight down Quinn's throat.

He didn't let a drop go to waste, only allowing Grady's cock to slip from his lips when it was softening a little and spent for the moment. Grady whimpered and leaned back, his head spinning, though it was a pleasant kind of dizziness that washed over him. Damn, maybe he should have had something more than a snack earlier, though it was a little late for that when he was warming in the afterglow, his legs trembling ever so slightly. Despite himself, he hoped Quinn would not notice, even if there was nothing there to be embarrassed about.

"Mmm, I didn't quite think you would go for that, but you can't blame a stallion from shooting his shot," Quinn chuckled, licking his lips as if he was savouring the lingering taste and residual aroma of Grady's musk in his mouth. "Mm… Come on, let's get you presentable again, darling, I don't want you being uncomfy out here."

Grady shivered.

"What about you though?" He said. "You haven't got off and you…"

He trailed off, half-shrugging, a small yet sheepish smile beginning to tug at his lips. It was obvious just how in need the other stallion was, though he wasn't at all sure just how big of a deal he should make about that.

"Nah, it's fine," Quinn said, shifting his legs apart a little more, as if it was not comfortable for him to walk with that tightness between them, his underwear keeping his cock just about in check at his sheath. "I'll see you later…or tomorrow, whenever we can, hm? It's enough just to spend time with you now."

He drew Grady into a hug, his bulge grinding up against Grady's softening cock, though that was almost enough to get the black and white stallion hard and throbbing all over again, practically swooning into Quinn's arms. Was he doing it deliberately? But, no, that wasn't at all any kind of game that Quinn played, not when he was as plain and as open as he was about things, sex and more. It was just an accident, if a happy one.

Grady, on the other hoof, was not quite ready at all to let Quinn go without some pleasure of his own.

With a flirty flick of his tail, he nipped at the stallion's neck, backing away from him, though he was only heading in closer to the barn wall.

"I don't want *you* to go without," he said pointedly. "You've already done so much for me... So, please... Let me take care of my stud too."

It made him blush hard to phrase it like that, yet turning his back on Quinn and casting him that shy look back over his shoulder clearly told Quinn all that he needed to know. The other horse's eyes widened sharply and he exhaled a breath in a puff of hot air, the bulge at his crotch seeming to grow. Yet that could have been Grady's overactive imagination at work.

"What... are you sure?"

It wasn't like Quinn to hold back, even though he was clearly desperate with need, when it came to his body, but that only endeared him even more to Grady. He loved that he wanted to make sure that he was okay and comfortable, that he wasn't feeling like he was being forced into anything. Not that he had ever been forced into anything like that, although it was not as if he had ever been with anyone that stepped up and took care of his needs quite like that before either.

It was what he needed and he whinnied softly, trying to be as quiet as he could as he turned to face the wall, pushing his backside out while he rested his forearms on it, putting an arch into his lower back. Quinn was only too keen, whispering to him in hushed tones to let him know if he wanted to stop at any time, to help him get his jodhpurs down over his buttocks – though only just enough to expose the round of his ass and his tail hole. No more needed to be exposed, not when what they were doing was already risk enough, Quinn drawing Grady down into the shaded part of the outside barn just a little more, where the branches of a leafy tree extended over them. It was not enough to disguise them both and what they were doing but it was enough to help a tiny bit.

"Unff… You really don't know how hot you are, do you, Grady?"

The stallion grunted, freeing his erection. He left his balls tucked back in his underwear too, though it was a shade easier for him to get his cock out than it was to expose Grady's dick. Grady didn't know that, however, not as he leaned heavily against the barn and relished in the sensation of the stud grinding into him, sliding his hard-on between his butt cheeks, up against the velvety dock of his tail.

"Ooooh, please…" He whinnied, surprising even himself. "I need you too…"

He was not one to beg, though perhaps what he was saying was a little more like communicating to Quinn what he needed from him. Quinn had never been one to hold back from what Grady wanted, always seeking to please and give as much as he took, pressing the head of his flat-tipped cock, with the meatier flare, to Grady's tail hole. Grady knew intimately in intricate detail just how that cock looked, the long, grey length with the flare that would be huge and bulbous at the point of orgasm, the wrinkles smoothing out… Yet that was not like feeling it sink into him, slowly but surely, his pucker softening around it as he did his best to relax around it. He didn't have to do much to get his body ready for Quinn, after all, yet it was always a shock to his system to feel that driving, slow penetration stretching him open more and more.

"Nnngghhhh…"

"Shit, Grady…" There was a laugh in Quinn's voice, despite the light admonishment. "Be quiet…"

But he couldn't be quiet, not completely, not when everything felt as good as it did, the hot length of meat driving into him, stretching him open a little more with every stroke. All until a good portion of the stud's cock, up far past the medial ring, was buried in his twitching tail hole, clenching around him without even thinking about it. The small notes of his body, just like that, came instinctively, his body wanting more and still not quite knowing what it was that it had to do to get it.

But it was okay. All he had to do was relax, to take every driving stroke of that cock as the medial ring pushed into him, tugging back and forth against his pucker. He swallowed a nicker as best he could, though it was not as easy as all that, huffing and grunting, his head swimming with lust. Even his nuts felt like they were aching and churning, even though it was mostly the pressure of his underwear and jodhpurs still pressing in on them, tucked away, that led him to that conclusion. It felt like there was too much stimulation all at once, the stallion shifting his weight from hoof to hoof and flipping his black tail up against Quinn's stomach in a desperate bid to relieve tension.

Grady's cock leaked as Quinn swore under his breath, his thrusts speeding up when the stallion would have usually taken his time. Of course, Quinn was more than aware of the need to be swift too and he wanted to savour every moment, even though they had to be speedy about everything.

Quick, so quick. Grady would make up for it later when they were alone and not having to worry at all about anyone walking in on them, thrust after thrust powering into him as he grunted, need coursing through.

"Unff... I... Uhhhhh!"

He groaned, muffling himself with his own hand pressed over his lips, need rising, the tight coil of desire in the pit of his stomach snapping like a predator. His spine chilled, though only for a moment, Quinn speeding up and up and up, though Grady was more than set already for a hands-free orgasm, long, thick jets of cum spurting forth, pouring into the dirt as the wilder splatters of cum shot up against the side of the barn. He was ejaculating, losing his load, before he was even aware of what was going on, what was happening, ecstasy flowing, throbbing, trying to kick back just to find some small way in which he could release that carnal need.

Yet all Grady could do, as his nostrils flared, was let himself go in pleasure, letting Quinn fuck him, roughly and crudely, like they were nothing more than two wild studs out there, taking their pleasure from one another. There would be so much more to come from their relationship and yet that night and that moment was just for each other, forgetting everything else and most certainly too the rest of the world. He huffed and grunted, letting his own muzzle go just to hang his head down against his arm, which had remained braced on the barn, quivering in place and flicking his tail up like a slut on show, as high as he possibly could for Quinn's pleasure.

Quinn, however, did not need any help, even though he had thrust Grady through a second, hoof-biting orgasm. He hammered in, the slap of his hips on Grady's buttocks louder than even their grunts, though it was not even in the stud stallion to hold back.

In all his glory, he let out a deep, long, guttural grunt that emanated up from the core of his being, swallowed down where his mind was still in its right place enough to remember that he had to be quiet. Hot spurts of thick stallion cream shot up under Grady's tail, right where it belonged, flowing deep, oozing out around the join of their bodies as Quinn kept right on thrusting and thrusting through the slick mess. The head of his cock flared out deliciously at the point of orgasm and, wonderfully, Grady was there to take it, though he would most certainly find himself more than a little sore when he came to taking care of the rest of his work for the day on the stable yard.

"Unff…"

Quinn leaned over Grady, though he still had to pull out, blinking quickly and glancing furtively around, in case there was something they had missed. Grady was barely even down from his own high, pleasantly shaky on his legs but not to the point that he didn't feel like he could walk yet, when Quinn was chuckling and ushering him, sloppily, back into his clothes like he'd never done before.

"Come on, come on," Quinn giggled, giddy in the aftermath of his climax. "Oh, god, I can't believe we did that!"

"I've never heard you like that before," Grady laughed, though he was just as bad, his ears twitching all over the place, tail flicking even as he tried to stuff his half-soft cock back into his underwear and jodhpurs. "Uh… It's not going in…"

But they found a way, some kind of way, to make it work, for they had gotten away with fucking on the stable yard at least that time. They didn't know for sure how many times more they could get away with something like that but, well…the first time had been what started it all off for the two of them, risking it all right there behind the barn.

The thrill of being exposed, exhibiting what they had to offer – and yet tucked away, all until they were ready to show who they were, out and proud. They would be more than happy to wait, though the stallions would find more places, just a few, to fuck and enjoy one another, taking a risk for the ultimate pleasure.

A quickie had never been quite so fun!

Shelter from the Storm

Jackson, more often than not known as Jack, could have watched Simon all day long. The stallion worked on the farm behind his house, which was a strange enough set up as it was, but he had studied out in the little university town in Wales and, well, he'd just stuck there. The houses up the hill from the small town backed on to fields and farmland, which was just how he had been able to watch Simon go about his work.

Simon… Simon was a pleasure to watch, though Jack should not have watched him as much as he did. It was just hard to ignore the rich, chestnut stallion when he was working, for he was so often visible from the kitchen window, all while Jack was doing the washing up. Or even when he was just hanging out in the garden, making the most of the space he had, the farm worker, though it turned out later that he had a stake in the family business of farming, stripping off his shirt to work at shearing the sheep.

Yes… With the sunshine glowing off his red brown coat, mane plastered to his neck with sweat as dark, sexy patches showed through his coat, the stallion was a joy to behold, someone that Jack could have drunk in, time after time again. Rippling with muscle, there barely seemed to be an ounce of spare fat on the stallion, though it was clear he built all that muscle from his work on the farm, all functional and needed. Not that Jack would have minded one little bit if it had all been from some form of vanity too. Who cared when someone looked that good, as long as they were happy and healthy?

Unlike Jack, who was a lightly built grey stallion on the studious side with a job in the archive library of the local university, Simon was built solidly. A stiff wind would struggle to push him over and Jack had seen him many times over working out in all kinds of weather, even heavy rain and tumultuous winds as the storms rolled in. Once, in passing, he had asked Simon why he did it, but the stallion had been as pragmatic as ever.

"I've got to get the animals looked after," he had said, as if there was nothing more to it than that. "They're not going to look after themselves, not when they don't have shelter. Besides, the sheep will be heavy with wool now, they'll be more comfortable if they don't get soaked through before we shear them."

It made sense and Jack admired Simon for his care and the patience that he had with all the animals he looked after. Of course, being Wales, there were lots of sheep around, though there were other animals too, like the small herd of cows that were apparently some kind of rarer breed, which he also milked. There were some goats too, a good number of turkeys and chickens, something that he called guinea fowl also. Jack was not much of an outdoorsy, "farmsy" stallion, yet Simon made him want to be that guy, even if he was sure too that he wouldn't have lasted all that long in that work.

No, he was much better sticking to his work in the library, amongst the books, even if his proximity to the bigger, more muscular stallion had him heading more often than before to the university gym (a perk of his job) just to make sure that he was looking after himself. Simon worked in the warmer weather without a shirt on, though he by far surpassed Jack when it came to physical prowess. And that was okay too, for they didn't need to be the same.

As the year moved into the summer months and they exchanged a few words, a few chats, even sharing a couple of drinks in Jack's garden – the little rental cottage that, thankfully, he had all to himself. Getting to know each other was slow because Jack didn't know whether he could just stroll over there and talk to Simon, even if that probably would have been okay. Maybe? He didn't know. Did guys do that still? And did Simon even know he was gay? He sometimes had a pride pin on and he thought he was kind of discreet about it… Not for any reason though, it was just the way he was, he didn't like to draw too much attention to himself, regardless of what he was wearing or where he was going. So bright colours and anything flashy or pointed that would have thrown more than a hint wasn't often on the table for him.

That was okay though. It was just… He was happy that way. If he changed in the future, he would change. Jack would be just the way he wanted to be and go forward, even if a couple of his friends had said that he should be more "out" than he was. What did that even mean?

Yet things with Simon, well… They were set to change, bit by bit, day by day. The small chats turned to Jack picking up a couple of things in the larger neighbouring town when he went down to get a new game, helping out from time to time, just with a few bits of paperwork and stuff. Apparently, Simon wasn't all that good at that kind of thing, though Jack was more than happy to help out when he had free time and waived any form of payment.

"It's like you're trying to keep me around," Jack had joked once, in the evening, when he had been settling up some accounts for Simon – not much, not that hard work. "There's always something… But it's always like that on the farm, isn't it?"

They'd laughed and talked that night and Jack had stumbled home pleasantly warm and tipsy, wondering if how the stallion's hand had rested on his knee had meant anything. Or if Simon had meant to let his hand linger like that…

Yet he didn't have to wonder for long, not when a storm rolled in a few days later. Jack frowned and eyed up the windows dubiously, for the one in the living room, looking out onto the back garden and over the wall to where Simon's farm was, didn't seal properly around the edge. It seemed to be okay for the moment, though there was always a chill in the living room due to it. That was why he didn't tend to use that part of the house in the winter months, though he had some papers set out on the coffee table at that time.

The knock on the door startled him, jumping and then pausing, heart hammering. Had it just been the storm? Yet the equine poked his head around into the hallway where he could see through the glass of the front door to the blurry, dark shape of someone on the other side. A muzzle pressed up to the glass and Jack gasped, rushing to the door. He knew that red brown face.

"Hey!" He puffed, wrenching open the door to reveal a dripping wet stallion, his mane plastered to his face and neck, tail hanging in rattails, all twisted up. "What's going on? Are you okay?"

Simon grunted and rubbed the back of his neck in an uncharacteristically sheepish fashion. For a moment, Jack feared that something was truly wrong.

"Hey," Simon said, offering Jack a friendly, lopsided smile. "Funny thing… I don't suppose you had a spare towel or something, do you? Got locked out of the house somehow when I was checking the sheep. Seems silly to smash a window when my brother should be home soon, you know? If you don't mind, that is."

Jack gulped, his ears splaying out, flopping to the sides of his head.

"Um, yeah, of course… Yes! Come in!"

Simon had never been inside his house – or rather, his small, one-storey cottage – before. That was new, even though it should not have been all that unusual, considering that he had been heading over to Simon's farm rather often of late to help him out, the strange, crackling connection between them growing and growing. Yet it was not natural to step back and let Simon inside, rushing off to get him the biggest towel that Jack owned, feeling as if he was fumbling and stumbling all over himself like a newborn foal. Just what was wrong with him?

Ah, but Jack knew, even as he held out the towel for Simon and watched, too intently, as Simon wrung out his mane and tail the best that he could, though his clothes were soaked through. Jack's heart hammered. Even though he had seen the stallion topless many times before, there was something about the way in which his shirt clung to his body, defining his pecs in particular, that just gave him the mental image of ripping it from Simon's body with relentless insistence in his mind.

No, you can't do that…

No, he could not. That would be rude, at the very least, and he just tried to think of what he could do to help Simon, rather than just stripping the poor horse down. He didn't even think Simon liked him "in that way" anyway and he didn't want to make things genuinely awkward between them when he had turned into such a good friend. But he couldn't have poor Simon just standing there, even though he was towelling off the best he could, dripping all over his carpet. That couldn't have been comfortable and, against himself, Jack shuddered, imagining just how uncomfortable Simon must have been with wet clothes clinging to his body. Yeah, that wasn't a sensation that Jack would have liked for himself either.

"Er, do you want…" He cast about for something that he could help with. "A shower? Something? Heh, I don't think my clothes would fit but…maybe there's some shorts or something I can lend you?"

Simon's gaze lingered on him, warm like liquid honey, for a long time. Though that could have been Simon's overactive imagination stretching the seconds out into more than what they were.

"Yeah," he said softly, in a voice that Jack had never heard before from him. "Yeah, that would be great… Thank you."

"Oh!"

Jack smiled, a wash of undue foolishness enveloping him, rubbing his neck, turning about. What was wrong with him?

"Great, then!" He said, his voice too high-pitched but there didn't seem to be anything that he could do about it. "Um… Yeah, I'll get the shower…running for you and, yeah, you can get in and everything…"

And then there was a hand on his arm, fingers sliding over his forearm gently, though they did not hold or stop him, not even as Jack's words died on his lips. Turning slowly, he locked his eyes with Simon's once more, the drumming of his frantic heartbeat nickering in his ears as if it had been trying to tell him something all along.

He's so close *to me…*

And would only be closer still. Jack stepped in, their chests nearly brushing, muzzles closer to one another than they had ever been before. Jack's tail swished, trying and failing to clamp down, his ears pricked forward, every last bit of his attention absolutely fixed on Simon. How could it not be?

"Jack…"

He breathed, though no words were needed, not as Jack froze, his lips slightly parted, the muzzle of the other equine coming in closer and closer to his. He was not paralyzed, not by any means, not as his heart sang, just afraid to break the moment, to lose what connection there was, to spoil what he couldn't believe was finally happening.

And, as awkward as he had felt when he had been trying to usher Simon into the cottage and get him dried off, everything came naturally, the stallion's hand rising to his face and curling tenderly around his cheek as their lips, finally, connected. The hand lingering on his knee, the other night, made sense, just one small part of a larger picture, and Jack whimpered faintly, light-headed, leaning into the kiss. Simon's lips moved against his as if they were meant to be there, so soft and so warm, and Jack leaned hungrily into it, without even realising what he was doing.

Simon grunted into the kiss and gripped his other arm at the biceps, though Jack had barely even realised that he had brought his arms up, getting them around the stallion, clutching at his clothes, his chest, just wanting him close. It was what he had wanted for so long and yet not known how to make a move or even if Simon swung that way, happy enough to at least have Simon's company even if there could be nothing more between them.

But it was more than that, so much more, all as Jack's shaking hands with the hoof-like, rougher fingertips fumbled at Simon's shirt. Some small part of his mind was still caught up in helping Simon get out of his clothes, yet neither horse was thinking about showering anymore. Not as the kiss deepened and Jack allowed the questing flick of Simon's tongue into his mouth, something inside him jolting as that fleshy, soft appendage swept up against his own. Investigating and experimenting with one another, as to what felt good, for the first time, Jack just about got a handful of buttons undone on Simon's shirt as he was backed up towards his bedroom. Thankfully for both of them, he had left the door to his bedroom ajar earlier that day, so Simon could, at the very least, see where they needed to go.

The next thing Jack knew was that he was tumbling back onto his bed in a flurry of limbs and laughing lips against his, giddy with delight.

"Fuck, I didn't think…" Simon grunted, breaking the kiss only to bury his face in the crook of Jack's neck, inhaling his scent deeply. "You… Mmm… So glad you didn't turn me down… Fuck…"

Jack giggled, a little more confident, helping Simon out of his shirt and letting out a needy little moan as more of that chestnut coat was revealed to him, darkened from the rain.

"I didn't think you swore that much," Jack teased, pushing Simon up just so that he could nip and nuzzle playfully at his neck, his blunter incisors catching and tugging at sensitive skin. "Maybe there's a lot I don't know about you."

The burning intensity in Simon's eyes, for a moment, made Jack wonder if he had said the wrong thing.

"I'll make you say my name like it's a swear, pony. I want to hear that from you, losing control and feeling *amazing*."

Jack whined, heart pounding, though that sounded like a good idea to him – a very good idea indeed. He was more than amenable to Simon stripping him down, both stallions fumbling and managing to work their way through, however haphazardly, getting each other's clothes off, down to their underwear. Yet it was Simon who drew down Jack's boxers, right there on his bed, to free the spring of his equine shaft to the light. It was mostly pink with a few blotches of grey around the base, which were more often than not hidden by his sheath, the soft fold of flesh that his cock would retreat into when he was soft.

His cock, in that moment, was anything but soft, however, Simon groaning as he closed his hand around it and watched Jack's face as his lips twitched and his ears splayed.

"Ooohhhh…"

Jack was almost embarrassed about the sound that came out of his mouth and yet it had every right to be there, very much so, as Simon kissed and nipped down Jack's body. Laying Jack back on the bed, he murmured something to him, something about wanting to make him feel good, and Jack whinnied something back. Words were hard.

But his agreement was there, especially as the stallion's lips closed around the head of his shaft, exploring his flare and sliding down, the warm, wet heat of a horse's long mouth closing around him. Jack nickered and let his head fall back with a loud huff, nostrils twitching and puckering as he struggled to drag in all the air he needed into his lungs.

"Ah… Ohhhh…"

"Mmmm, just relax… Tell me if you don't like something…or if you like something… Hmm…"

Simon took his time with him; at least, that was how it felt to Jack. It was as if he was the most important stallion, or thing, in the world to Simon at that time, as if the rest of the world and perhaps even the farm beyond the walls had ceased to exist. And yet Jack would not have begrudged Simon in the slightest if he had ducked out, at any point, to tend to the farm or any other incidents due to the storm or something else. Because that was just the kind of guy that Simon was and that was why Jack liked him as much as he did, all in how the stallion put those in his care above his own needs.

The stallion's lips slid down more and more over his cock, taking Jack's dick in up to the medial ring while he caressed the remaining length with his hand, working up and down. He tested Jack's reactions with little squeezes, taking his cock easily into the back of his throat as he sank all the way down, taking him fully to the sheath. Jack moaned, his hands suddenly on the horse's head, fingers tangling into his mane as if he was afraid that it was at that very moment that Simon was going to disappear, no longer even exist at all.

"Mmm…"

The stallion hummed around his length and Jack squirmed as those vibrations travelled into his body. They were not the sort of thing that would have gotten him off, but they were different and that night was all about new things, though he had, of course, been with a guy before. Never with another stallion, however, and never with anyone who knew how to make his heart pound and his stomach lurch in quite that delightful way.

All he could do was moan, trying to tell Simon, without the luxury of coherent words, just how much he adored everything he was doing, that he couldn't wait to make him feel good too, a leg twitching while he strove to take it all in. Every moment was precious, after all, from how Simon cradled his thick shaft on his tongue, pressing the fleshy width of it to the underside, and the smooth slide of his long muzzle up and down, working Jack up more and more. There could be no better muzzle, let it be said, than that of an equine anthro for sucking cock, though many were far more infatuated with their dicks to even get down to that.

Of course, Jack wasn't out to objectify anyone, even though he was very much enjoying the moment, huffing and grunting, panting lightly, his head swirling with too much emotion colliding with lust to even function. His body took over for him, tightening his grip with one hand in Simon's mane and rolling his hips up to meet him. Simon groaned as his lips forced Jack's sheath to wrinkle back just a little more, need flaring up thick and fast between the stallions.

It had to come out, yet Jack could already feel that tightening in his body, that sense of urgent need that meant it was *coming*. He moaned and rolled his head from shoulder to shoulder yet, even then, Jack didn't even have the heart to think about anything else at all, not when his body sung with heat and he wanted to get off so badly. To have that high and that special, vulnerable moment with Simon was all that his desire had been craving for so long. He didn't have the strength in him to deny himself that, even as the skin over the larger muscles near the surface of his body twitched and jumped in that uniquely equine fashion.

"Mmmph… Ohhh!"

He was close, so very close – yet Simon did not allow it, not quite yet. Jack whinnied and shot him a plaintive look, almost accusatory, though Simon only chuckled and kissed the flared head of his cock as he drew back. The flare had thickened up noticeably, for Jack had really been that close to climax, yet neither stallion minded truly, not as the thick meat of Simon's dick tented out his boxer briefs, which had not yet been tugged off.

"I just wanted to ask…first…" Simon breathed, huffing and puffing faintly, trying to get his breath back. "Oof… Could I…cum inside you? Fuck, you make me… Ah, I don't mean to swear… You just make me want you so bad."

Simon blushed and Jack couldn't have denied him anything, not even in that moment, even if he'd wanted him to.

"Ah… You can," he said, hesitating slightly, though only because he wanted to find the right words. "I just…haven't had anything inside me for a while, not been playing like that. Is that okay? It'd be slow, you know…"

"More than okay."

The husky warmth rolling through Simon's tone warmed Jack all the way through and he nickered throatily before the other stallion's lips closed on his own again. They kissed deeply, Jack's tongue more boldly darting forward to toy with and play against Simon's, though they could have kissed however they liked. There was no right way nor any wrong way to kissing, after all, and they moaned deeply, letting their lust guide them.

Jack tugged down Simon's underwear as they were kissing and the stallion broke the kiss with a chuckle to get them all the way off. Right there and then, a beautiful beast of a cock was revealed, hard and throbbing with the passion of a stallion, unusually mottled from flare to base, ducking into the sheath, in pink and grey. There was no telling quite what the base colour of his cock should have been, either way, and, frankly, it didn't matter at all. Not as Jack closed his hand around it, marvelling at the thickness and blushing hard, his ears tipping back softly.

"You're bigger than me," he grunted, though it was not a bad thing. "I don't know… I'm gonna try to take you, okay? There's lube in the little dresser… The one…over there."

There was a single beside table, with three drawers, beside Jack's bed, though he was sure that Simon had barely been focusing on taking in his bedroom at all when he had been backing Jack into it. Not that Jack minded, enjoying the moment to relax a little, his heartbeat simmering down softly, watching Simon's profile as his forelock dried on his face. Simon seemed mostly dry already, though there were still some dark patches on the short coat of hair covering his body that betrayed dampness still. Jack would more than take care of that afterwards for him, though he was sure that that too would require a shower and drying off all over again…

"Ah, I see it," Jack said triumphantly, after a moment of rummaging. "I'll be really gentle, we don't have to go all the way if you're too tight, it's all okay…"

Yet it was intimate, so very much so, for Jack to lift his legs, lying on his back, for Simon to prepare the pucker of his tail hole for such attention. It was not something that was necessary, not by any means, for any anal penetration, though it was something that relaxed him and helped him ease the muscles around there as the stallion softly spread a generous helping of lube over and into his hole. Simon slipped a single digit inside and Jack whickered anxiously, though it was easy to take, gentle enough that he even caught himself bucking his hips and grinding back on it, just a little.

"Mmmph…"

"It's okay, just take it easy… There's no rush."

"Maybe for you," Jack muttered, trying to be flirtatious, but not sure how he was coming off. "I want it too…"

Simon smiled and nickered softly – a gentle sound that Jack was only too keen to return to him. His finger twitched inside, working back and forth to relax him, though it did have the added effect of easing his muscles, the gentle stroke encouraging them to relax. For that was the most important thing about anal sex, after all, and not the lube, even if that helped a lot mentally. And Jack liked the foreplay, the quivering, tingling feeling of being looked after and taken care of, though he was far from fragile. At least, that was his opinion on the matter.

Jack moaned, lying back, his legs hitched up towards his chest and his knees bent. It was a strange sort of exposure to have the thick flesh of his doughnut exposed to Simon, especially when it was just their first time together, though a part of sex included the details that perhaps were not thought about when fantasising. Even as heat spread across his muzzle and to the insides of his ears, he laid there, turning his head into the pillow where he had scooted up the bed a little and letting the cool soothe his face.

"You're doing so well," Simon murmured, adding a second finger, though he seemed to enjoy the experience as much as Jack, a goofy smile keeping his lips a little stretched even then. "You're going to take me so well…"

"Mmmph, stop," Jack grumbled, blushing harder and burying his face, as much as he could, into the pillow. "You're going to make me die of embarrassment over here."

"When I'm telling you how good you are, that should never happen."

Simon twisted his stomach up into knots so very easily, as if it all came naturally to the stallion, something that he did not have to think about in the slightest. Jack whimpered, though he still wanted Simon to keep going, especially as he worked his fingers back and forth and teased them up against his prostate. There could be no doubt as to when that part of his sensitive anatomy had been teased as Jack's legs twitched and his cock throbbed, drooling a little more pre-cum, milkier and thinner than before. That had always been the way for Jack, however, when he had done some prostate play on himself, having thinner cum if he made himself climax from that alone.

It was not about that, however, not as his cock throbbed and the flared tip, which had not grown smaller or softened, drooled more and more pre-cum, forced out as Simon worked his fingers back and forth. The stallion curled his fingers to better stimulate Jack's prostate, pressing down on that button and twisting his hand, experimentally, back and forth, just to see what angle worked best for him, what made Jack quiver the most deliciously.

"Ah... P-please..." Jack moaned, almost stuttering. "I need it... I need to cum."

Simon smiled and slipped his hand back, wiping it off on a shirt that was discarded there, though that could always be washed later.

"I wouldn't want to keep you waiting, hon..."

He spoke as if they were already more familiar with each other than they were, though Jack didn't mind that at all. In fact, to him, it rather felt like coming home to something soft and familiar, despite everything.

He could get used to that. Especially as Simon pressed over him, not bending his legs back too far but allowing his hooves to kick out to the sides so that the stallion had room to move into, to press the head of his exposed cock up to the prepared, slick bud of Jack's tail hole. The grey equine quivered and moaned, though Simon bent his long neck down just enough to get their lips to brush, the kiss of breath tickling each other's lips just as intimate as a true, lustful press of their lips together would have been.

He was ready. Or as ready as he would ever be. But that didn't stop him from craving it, his heart longing for something that he had never felt from Simon before, as if not getting it would change the course of his life forever. He huffed and panted, letting Simon take a moment to line up his cock properly – and then relaxed as much as he could as the stallion pressed into him.

The head popped inside and Jack moaned, head spinning, flat back on the pillow, the heat from his body prickling all over as he sweated lightly. The musk of the stallions, together, filled the air as they moaned and grunted, Simon bearing in slowly, allowing Jack to savour every inch as it stretched him open. One inch after another of that delectable, thick cock, a good three inches at least longer than his own was, spread him open, demanding entry as he even tried to squirm on it, needing more.

"Ah! Yesss… Ohhhh!"

"Mmm, oh, wow… You feel…" Simon grunted, his eyes half-lidded, nose twitching, seeming to struggle with something. "So…good…"

Jack was more than happy to hear that, nickering back softly and bumping his muzzle with Simon's though there was only so close that he could get without bending himself up uncomfortably from the bed. No… It was better to sink into sensation, to enjoy his tightness being stretched and spread, his muscles introduced to a length of cock that was new to his body in many ways. He panted softly, dragging in all the air he could through his nostrils, though every hot breath that he expelled washed down over Simon's neck and chest as he tucked his head down, trying to grapple with the overload of pleasure.

For it was good, hotter than he could have imagined, the slick slide of that cock into him letting him fall into the moment, to forget that there ever had been a time at all where Simon had not been right there in bed with him. Nothing else mattered, not as he gripped Simon's shoulders for something to stabilise him there, whimpering and grunting, his legs bending a little further back still, knees close to his chest, so that Simon could get a better angle, thrusting in a little deeper. The medial ring popped in past his strained anal pucker and Jack cried out wordlessly, his cock hard and twitching on his stomach.

That had never happened before. As with many that tried anal penetration, he didn't always have the ability to keep his dick hard throughout the whole thing, which was more than normal. It was something about the pleasure and the pressure doing it for him – yet, that time, his dick was nearly hard the whole time. As Simon thrust, slowly and gently, working him open and used to his cock, his shaft still throbbed and pulsed, even if it did not have quite enough firmness in it to jerk up from his belly.

With Simon grasping it, as soon as he was securely buried within Jack's backside, the horse didn't have it in himself to care at all. All he wanted was for Simon to keep thrusting and filling him forever, nickering for more, even stubbornly insisting that he could take more than what the stallion was giving him.

Simon smirked and let Jack have it – just a bit more. A couple more delicious inches and then a harder thrust, a pounding of his hips, testing his resolve and just what he could take. Yet he was not about to find Jack slipping, no, not in the slightest, not as he took every stroke like a pro, for it was always the initial penetration that he had struggled the most with when it came to that kind of play.

"Agh, oh… Yes… More…" He nickered, his eyes on Simon even as his lower jaw fell slightly slack, no longer even having the energy to keep his mouth closed when it just didn't matter anymore. "I need… Oh… Yes… Please…"

"I got you, little stud, I got you. Damn, your ass… Mmm!"

Simon ploughed him, breath hitching and catching, hot swathes of it washing over Jack on the bottom while they shared their lust and their desire mounted increasingly. He moaned loudly, his legs aching from where they had been pushed back, hamstrings stretching, though he didn't have it in himself to care. What did it matter when everything felt as damn good as it did? He was there for the moment and only that, grunting and moaning, whimpering, twisting his hips back and forth to the small amount that he could, trapped lusciously under the bigger stallion's muscle.

And yet he felt protected, as if being under Simon was exactly the place he needed to be, his tail hole burning a little from the stretch, though he was more than willing to go through that little of discomfort for the pleasure to come. He groaned long and low, not caring that he was being more vocal than he had ever been. It was funny just how many things seemed to go out of the window when it came to Simon and the relationship that had been building even though Jack hadn't been at all sure whether there was anything there between them.

Thankfully for him, he had been wrong. And Jack had never been as glad as he was to be wrong, taking every stroke as Simon, finally, sank every inch of horse cock that he had to give into his tight ass. Jack grunted, his cock throbbing within the grasp of Simon's hand, though the stallion wasn't jerking him off yet, letting him take in every moment.

"Oh, fuck… *Simon*…"

"Unff…" Simon grunted, eyes twinkling. "I told you I'd make you say my name, unff…like a curse."

Jack would have playfully smacked him for that quip if he had been in any kind of position to do so, yet the moment was not right for that. And that was okay, all very much so, as Simon thrust and thrust, the long, rolling strokes of his cock powering deeply into the stallion and claiming him.

Yet orgasm had to come eventually and Jack grunted as it stirred in his loins again, though the tight cord of need within him had been present for quite some time already. He squirmed and twitched and yet, wonderfully so, there was nowhere for him to go as he took every stroke, panting and moaning. The horse's ears twitched and he closed his eyes, sinking into the moment, squeezing and clenching around Simon if only for a second, just to feel how it was, how he could make that tightness even more deviously delectable.

"Nnnggghhhh…"

He groaned. He was close, so close, Simon's hand working over his cock, pumping up and down, all the way up to just below the flare and then back down again. The rhythm was quick, the telltale "fwap" sound of a hand moving over a cock filling the air – that was, of course, if the slap of his hips on Jack's round rump, muscle contracted, didn't dominate all else. And the hot huff and pant of stallion breath, the grunts and groans winding into one another, as if they had merely been waiting for a moment in which they could make themselves known.

"Cum for me," Simon grunted, encouraging him, his voice dropping an octave so that it was even sexier and throatier than before. "Mmmph… Fuck… I'm…"

But Jack knew it too as he arched his back and neighed, the sound cutting through the air, ecstasy flooding him. His balls let loose everything that he had to give and there was no holding back at all in a moment like that, not for him, not as he let it flow and flow and flow. Long, thick spurts of creamy cum, a little milkier than would have been normal for him from the anal play, splattered his stomach, hitting just below his chest. He had never been one to get serious reach with his cum shots, yet the warm spatter of cream marking his own grey body sent a carnal thrill through him like nothing else had.

Simon was about to show him that there were things, however, that could be even better than that as his thrusts sped up, his eyes on Jack. Jack knew that he was still checking in with him, making sure that everything was okay, but Jack wasn't about to tell him he had clenched so hard at the point of climax that everything felt a lot tighter than it had before. Even if there was a greater flare of strain within his aching passage, he was not about to stop, not when he could have every drop of his partner's load throbbing up under his tail.

The stallion moaned, leaning far over him, unconsciously putting more and more pressure on Jack's legs, though Jack didn't care. The soreness would be a pleasant reminder, come morning, of all the fun that they had enjoyed that night, when the course of their lives had changed forever.

So, he wanted to take it, as the strokes of the stallion's cock sped up and up, losing himself while Jack was right there, ready and waiting, to catch him.

Finally, as Jack's cock lay half-soft against his lower abdomen, Simon lost control. He tucked his head down, bending his neck into a shiny curve, grunting deep in the back of his throat, his jaw clenched and eyes closed. The first hot spurt of cum ploughed up into Jack's backside, though the horse was not sure just how much of that he was imagining and how much he could actually feel from the thick flare buried in his rump. Either way, it was better than he could ever have imagined, grabbing the horse's face and rubbing the tension from his cheek and the muscles above his eyes that controlled the action of the jaw, soothing what he could.

"Mmmm… Let it all out, stud."

That didn't sound like anything that should have ever come from Jack's mouth, but all was well and good, for it felt like him, even if it did not sound like him. And he could let it be, breathlessly kissing the softness of Simon's nose and his arms where he leaned far over him, though Jack could only just about reach his shoulders. That was the problem with the position, alas, though spooning or doggystyle would not, most likely, put them in any closer proximity for kissing and sweetness.

They would just have to experiment, playing back and forth, trying out new things to see what worked for them. Jack couldn't *wait*.

He grunted, laying back, a soft smile spreading more across his face, as if his lips rebelled against the mere notion of returning to a neutral position. It was just too good, dribbles of cum leaking sensually back out along the line of his partner's dick, oozing where their bodies were joined. A dull ache spread through him from his tail hole and yet Jack still kept that to himself, even if things would end up, once again, with Simon taking care of him later and making sure he was, once again, comfortable. Once they had fucked a few times, he would get used to the stretch again anyway. And even Simon could bottom too, swapping back and forth for the pleasure of it all.

The storm raged outside as Simon, slowly, as if he didn't really want to, slipped free of Jack's tail hole, the flare so thick that it had to lightly tug a couple of times at his clenched ring in order to make its way free. The thick, pink flare had swollen to almost twice its size

– definitely a grower at the point of orgasm when it came to the flare – but his cock would prove to take quite a long time to deflate fully.

It was a good thing indeed that the two stallions had time – all the time in the world for one another, in fact. For they had found a slower way of life out there in the countryside, both on the edge of the town with the local, quiet facilities at their disposal and access to the nearby towns by car most easily. There was a world out there for them to explore, when the time was right for them to go together, yet they would still find themselves, time after time again, snuggled up together after a long day of work with a bottle of wine and a raging, crackling fire to warm them through.

And the bed would be warm too, when they were both in it together, tangled in stallion grunts and groans, pleasure upon pleasure rising with the throb of their shafts. But there was so much more to it than that for Jack and Simon.

As Simon held him, letting Jack rest his head on his chest, Jack's lips parted softly, his eyelids heavier and heavier. He'd hated before how he always wanted to drop off to sleep after sex but, well, that was just what happened sometimes and wasn't a bad thing, not when he was with Simon. Not when the storm battered the windows and threatened to rip tiles from the roof, for he had Simon right there with him, his big, muscled body everything he could ever have wanted to protect him.

The soft rise and fall of the stallion's chest lulled him to doze: a light nap until they decided they needed to go clean up in the shower. But a couple of beers, what Jack had left in the house, and a good show on TV they could laugh too would go a long way to wrapping up the stormy night to such a point that Simon would not even want to go home when his brother realised he had been locked out.

In taking shelter from the storm, the stallions opened the door to something new.

Down by the Canal

"I don't know why you wanted to go out tonight… Down here, of all places?"

Simon grunted and snorted, the stallion huffing as he tossed his head, flipping his long, grey forelock out of his eyes. Logan had dragged him out after dinner, and rather a filling dinner at that, for a stroll down the canal. It was not actually all that far from Logan's place, it had to be said, but Damon had never been all that much of an outdoorsy colt or stallion. He was much more frequently found perched at the computer when he was not working, delving into different games and exploring new fandoms. At the very least, it took a lot to keep his attention.

Logan chuckled, holding a low hanging tree branch out of the way, even though Damon was a few inches shorter than him.

"The walk will do you good," he snorted, good humour dancing in his eyes. "You know that. Didn't the doctor advise more cardio?"

Damon grunted and grumbled, tail swishing behind him. Yeah, Logan was right, but that didn't mean one bit that the horse had to like it, no way. He was happy with his lifestyle the way it was and, honestly, he didn't eat too much junk anyway. He was almost vegetarian with the manner in which he preferred to eat, rarely consuming meat products. Some herbivores were like that though, their digestive systems still more finely tuned to digest plant products rather than meat, even though they were anthros and mostly able to. Logan, however, was known to devour a burger on frequent occasion.

Damon chose not to say anything back to that, tipping his chin up a little higher as he flicked his tail, striking Logan on his bare thigh. He had to admit, it was nice to see his boyfriend out in shorts – shorter than they needed to be, really, because Logan was just that bulky. His thighs were thick and clearly defined with muscle. Even though the draft horse tended to get a lot fluffier in winter with a thick coat of hair, it was still short in his summer garb, a little moulting away already in late August. Damon didn't really shed all that much of his coat, being a finer, lighter type of equine anthro.

He spared a moment, however, to glance appreciatively at Logan's calves and thighs, raking his gaze up the stallion's muscular body, beyond the dark brown hair, revealing a rich, deep bay coat. The brown of his hair was so rich that he could very nearly be classed as a liver chestnut, yet he still had that distinction between his mane and tail and his body, the black hair spilling down his chunky neck as if it was tempting the eye to follow it.

"Hmph…"

Damon shook himself. He couldn't get caught up in looking at his boyfriend like that, not when they were out in public. It was already evident just what an effect the bigger, stronger stallion had on him, as his sheath plumped out within his boxer briefs, swelling and thickening, trying to release his cock even then.

He walked ahead, his eyes tentatively on the water and a lazy canal boat chugging by them. They always seemed so slow… He didn't think he would enjoy being on one all that much. Sure, it was a different way of seeing the English countryside, but he liked, at least, to be up and moving. Even if slowly…and walking…

Okay, so maybe being on a canal boat wouldn't have been as terrible as anything else, but Damon was just trying to distract himself with the lure that was his boyfriend. There was a little fleck of white on the stallion's shoulder, concealed by his loose vest top at that moment where the strap lay, but he knew it was there. Damon's lips had been on that spot only a short time ago, the night before, kissing and nipping and teasing until Logan pinned him down and fucked him in just the way he liked to be fucked.

Damn, he was horny… Damon resisted the urge to shiver, though his tail still tensed and clamped down. He only just resisted the urge to pin his ears back; the instinct to do so was buried so deeply that he often did it, and other little things like that, without even thinking twice about it.

Logan, of course, caught the look. The stallion pretended not to see, though he still gave a flirty swish of his tail, accidentally-on-purpose brushing it against the back of Damon's calves. Even though Damon was wearing his jeans, a little too tight and showing off his ass perfectly, the smaller stallion shivered.

That's right, darling, he thought to himself, hiding his smirk by tilting his head away from his partner. *You know what you want…*

Logan, truly, was just there to facilitate it. After all, what need did he have to force the issue on anything? He was grateful that he could rest assured in the knowledge that Damon would always tell him if he didn't want to do something or if he wanted to stop. He needed to know that someone would always tell him if he went too far or gripped them too tightly, too concerned with his strength. Yet there had been some slip-ups in his younger days that, ultimately, Logan didn't want to repeat, not ever.

The grey stallion snorted and whuffled, the pink spot on his nose twitching as he grinned.

"So, now that you're done getting me out of the house," Damon quipped, a hand propped up on his hip, "are you going to tell me where you're taking me?"

Logan smiled more softly at that, his ears splaying out and then flicking forwards, pricking to attention. It was impossible for him not to pay attention to Damon.

"No, hon," he said, bumping his partner gently with his hip as he caught up to him. "That would take all the fun out of it."

Damon grunted.

"Jeez…"

It was good-natured, however, and Damon fell into stride along with Logan. Logan's legs were longer than Damon's, but he shortened his stride enough so that they were not walking too much out of sync. His hooves dug into the soft loam with every step, barefoot and not bothering with even the type of boots that equine anthros could most easily wear. But barefoot hooves were better at gripping, the bars on them running down alongside the frog, though there was a natural sense of being able to feel the ground through the hoof too.

Damon couldn't help but be glad that horseshoes had fallen out of fashion since they had started cutting up and scraping indoor floors, once anthros had evolved into a more civilised society, centuries back. In evolution came changes, even with society learning and evolving rather than in their physical bodies.

"You look like you're thinking very hard about something," Logan teased, pressing in close, bumping Damon with his shoulder, though he nudged him away from the water, towards the trees bordering the canal path. "What's on your mind?"

The stallion grinned widely in a flash of white teeth.

"Just about how sexy you'd look in a pair of shiny horseshoes. They'd have to be clip-on ones though, we're not nailing anything into your hooves."

Logan chuffed a laugh, his nostrils fluttering.

"Why not? It won't hurt."

"But it'd affect your gait, how you walk and all that," Damon added, waving his hand dismissively, though Logan seemed to be very close to him all of a sudden. "I don't want to hurt you, it was a silly thought."

"I know, I know, I was just teasing," Logan made a point of saying, even though it was all still light-hearted banter between them. "But I'd wear a pair of sexy boots or clip-on shoes any day for you, you should know that."

"Mm, I do like that thought…"

The colt hesitated for a moment, halfway through his stride. It was only a breath of a moment, no more than that, but it was enough, more than enough for Logan to slide his hand around him, his hot breath on Damon's neck. Squeaking, Damon half-turned to Logan, but the bigger stud was too quick for him, bearing him back under the branches. Damon grunted as a scratchy, short branch caught at his T-shirt, though the bite and the scrape of pressure was short-lived as a warm hand pressed over his crotch.

And then Damon stopped thinking – clearly, at least. Logan pressed his hand, rolling from the heel of his hand to his fingers and back again, over his crotch, teasing and changing the amount of pressure that he used. He gripped the base of Damon's sheath, teasing and sliding his fingers up to where the swelling pressure of the stallion's cock flowed up, trying to find release and somewhere to escape to.

"What – Logan?" Damon all but yelped, stifling his cry just in time. "What are you doing? Logan!"

But the stallion was not to be forced away so easily, not when Damon was pressing himself into him, as if by shoving Logan backwards, rather ineffectively, he was going to stop the stallion from groping his rising hard-on in public. Well, it wasn't really "in public" per se, not when there was no one else around, though Damon was all too aware that it hadn't been all that long since the canal boat had passed them.

"Why?" Logan teased, though he released the pressure on Damon's crotch, the grey colt grunting and shuddering in place, holding back the urge to thrust his hips up into his boyfriend's grip. "Tell me if you want me to stop. I won't go any further until you tell me, I won't push."

Damon's head spun. It was hard to think straight when it felt like every drop of blood in his body had rushed to his crotch. The stallion panted, puffing in and out quick breaths through his nostrils, lips pressed together, though his muzzle still twitched a little, his nerves on fire.

"Mmph..." Damon shook his head, eyes half-closed, his hands somehow weakly up against his boyfriend's chest. "I didn't... I don't want to stop..."

It was hard to say the words aloud and yet it was imperative he did, that he got them all out, one way or the other. He didn't want, after all, anything to be misconstrued, not when things had been going as well between them as they had been. No one had been taught explicitly to communicate well and that had been something that they had both tried to improve and get a grip on early in their relationship.

So, things had to be clear, even though there was heat in his cheeks and his loins, swelling and thickening, his cock rising attentively into the tantalising press of Logan's hand. It could have been nothing at all, just a tease for something more, yet he needed it, ached for it, moaning desperately as he failed to stifle his cries of delight.

"Ooh... Mmph!"

"You're a vocal little colt this evening, aren't you?"

Damon squirmed. It had all happened so quickly! And yet he didn't want things to come to a halt, no, not at all. He wanted to play out everything, to see just where things were going to go, lusting for something that was spiralling well out of his control and into the control of another. He licked his lips, ears twitching, trying to retain control over himself... However, it just wasn't happening. It was not intended to happen, no, not in any way. But it was and his heart sung for it, a long, low groan parting his lips all over again.

And Logan was right there for them both, making sure that everything was alright. He dropped a tender kiss on Damon's forehead, nuzzling in close, and the colt whined, folding right into Logan's arms. After all, it was right where he belonged.

"There's a good pony..."

Damon shuddered. Oh, that hit all the right notes inside him. Especially as Logan tugged at his jeans, so tight, showing off his ass and thighs, yet freeing his sheath and swelling erection, nonetheless.

"You..." He struggled to breathe, let alone to talk, huffing and panting heavily. "You... What if someone comes by? What if they see?"

He didn't know if anyone was actually going to come by and catch them in the act, but it didn't really matter. He was too far gone anyway, knowing exactly what he wanted as he gulped and groaned, leaning in heavily against Logan. The stallion supported him, tucking him in amongst the branches and leaves, all so he didn't have to keep himself held up.

"No one will see," Logan said, reassuring him even as he hushed him. "Don't worry... I've got to take care of you when you're this needy, you know..."

The pony grunted, squirming. Sometimes he felt the size difference between them even more than usual, though he hissed through his teeth as the stallion's skilled hand closed around his cock, working it up and down. He pumped his hand up and down, grasping and holding his cock, smoothing his rough hand over it, even though the hair coating the palm was lightly coassr where it had taken the most friction over the years. That Logan often lifted barbells and dumbbells at the gym, sometimes with rougher knurling on the larger bars, meant it had been scraped up a little recently, more than usual.

But Damon loved it. There was nothing like the touch of his partner, how he felt holding his shaft, sliding his hand up and down, from the crinkling of the sheath where it tried to pull back to expose even more of his cock to the flared tip. Of course, the head was flatter, at that moment, though not so flat the edges of the flare could not be seen, thickening up as if he was working towards cumming already.

"Ah-ah-ah," Logan admonished playfully, letting Damon whimper and tuck his nose in against his neck. "Not so quickly… You don't have to always cum so quickly, you know…"

He squirmed again, a delicious shiver running through his body. He needed it and yet it was better, undoubtedly, when Logan was in control. When Logan took charge, he didn't have to worry about anything else, letting himself be swept away, even in the devious thrill of exhibitionism. He didn't really know if they would be caught there at all, of course, but he didn't even know if he wanted to be caught either, whether he wanted that horrifying realisation that there was someone there watching them fuck, someone that was perhaps as turned on by watching them play out there in the open as they were to be observed in the moment.

He didn't know. What Damon did know, however, was that it made him hotter than ever, his skin crawling and prickling with desire, need rolling through him with beat after beat of his heart. Some things, after all, could not be set aside quite so easily, and his tail flagged as thick bubbles of pre-cum oozed from his cock, the head flaring out even more, plumper around the edges.

"Mmmph... You make it so..." Damon wriggled. "Hard... Hard to hold back."

"Then maybe you should take a break, show me what that slutty, wonderful mouth of yours can do, darling."

"Oh..."

Logan smiled at how easily Damon folded to his knees and the ground. His cock was still out, but that didn't seem to matter anymore, hanging down softly as the head tried to follow the pull of gravity. It was too hard, however, to pull down fully, throbbing and twitching with need.

And Logan was more than happy to satisfy that need, bit by bit and moment by moment. It only had to come in time. There was only so much the two of them could do all at once and he hadn't dragged poor Damon all the way down the canal path to look at the view, as nice as that had been.

Damon was good, gently fishing out Logan's cock, blushing as his ears folded back and down to the sides, softly and smoothly. It was easy once he got into it and Damon languished there, letting the moment roll through him, forgetting they were out in public. The ground under his knees was a little soft and he had to admit, even then, it was a little uncomfortable to kneel in damp soil, almost mud, but he didn't care. His jeans were too tight and yet he would have gone through it all many times over, as long as it meant that he got to please his partner.

Getting his own rocks off in the process was just a happy by-product of them getting into something a little kinkier.

I can't believe I'm doing this…

The stallion's eyelids flickered, peering up through his eyelashes as he ducked his muzzle down more than a little shyly and looked up at the beast of Logan's cock as it was revealed. The stallion left his nuts tucked back and away in his underwear, the two of them still mostly clothed, yet it would have been clear, of course, to anyone walking by just what the horses were up to. He grunted and licked his lips, parting them willingly for the monster of his boyfriend's cock.

Because there was nothing quite like taking that long, thick length into his mouth, gulping it down and taking the fat head into the back of his throat. He didn't have a gag reflex, being an equine, so he didn't have to worry about that, not as he closed his eyes and devoured the fat shaft.

"Unff… Ah, you're always so good at that, little colt…"

Logan's warm words of praise washed over him and Damon shivered, simply unable to help himself. Damn it, why did being told that he was good just feel so, well…good? It was hard to string words together in the right order to form a coherent thought in his mind, though it didn't matter. The length of Logan's meat was mostly grey with some tiny, pink flecks around the flare on the side that was harder to see when he was fully engorged. If his sheath was pushed back just a little more, there was a spot of pale pink on his shaft, tucked away down there, that could be seen too.

But Damon was more wrapped up in taking Logan's flare down into his throat, gulping and swallowing around him. Even though he was well-practised at taking the draft horse's cock after so long, it still made his eyes water for the first few moments he did it. But that was okay, as long as he relaxed into it, grunting and groaning lightly, his tail trying to flag. With it being looped through the hole and fastening in the back of his jeans, however, it didn't move too much or threaten to reveal his backside.

It was strange to take Logan's cock when he was still as clothed as he was, everything closing in around him, as if his attire was squeezing his body. Damon whined and squirmed, nostrils fluttering as a hint of an annoyed nicker floated out.

"Mmph…"

"There you go, little pony," Logan crooned to him, his voice barely above a whisper. "You can take it, colt, just swallow again. You're doing so well for me."

That was more than enough to steal Damon's attention from anything that may have been crowding or distracting him. Who cared if there was damp seeping through his jeans into his knees? Did it really matter if a drop of water, from the tree branches above, fell on his head? The soft crispness of a recent rainfall hung in the air and he breathed in deeply and slowly, relishing in the sense of grounding that it offered him.

And then there was the trickle and bubble of the water in the clear canal flowing behind him. They were not all that far from the canal and barely even off the path, though Damon was too far gone to worry. All he felt was a shocking tingle in his body, as if every nerve ending had suddenly become ten times more sensitive than they had been before, his skin crawling with an inviting electricity. If he hadn't known better, Damon would have said that there were a hundred imaginary fingers tracing over his body, every part, bringing a fresh rise of need to his aching, throbbing cock.

"Mmph…"

He groaned around the cock in his mouth, angling his head so that Logan could more easily plough and grind into his throat with a steady roll of his hips. There didn't seem to be any rush at all to Logan's pace, allowing Damon to relax into it as he cradled the meaty length on his tongue. He could not lap, not when Logan was taking charge like that, so he kept his eyes closed and focused on the moment as much as he could, sinking into it, absorbing every tiny detail.

Like how smooth Logan's dick felt sliding by the tight seal of his lips.

The lingering taste of ever so slightly bitter pre-cum at the back of his mouth, just about gracing his tongue.

The lustful shudder that went through his partner as Logan rammed deep, teasing Damon's nose all the way up to the wrinkle of his sheath.

"Oof… Yes…"

Even Logan had to give in to lust, sooner or later, though it had never been the stallion's intention to cum too quickly. He'd spent a little time checking out the canal path beforehand and was fairly sure no one would be by – but there was always that risk. Huffing hotly, his nostrils flared, the stallion tried to keep an eye on the path behind Damon, but that was something that was very much more easily said than done. Especially when his dear colt's lips swept around him like that, his tongue twitching and flicking to the small extent that it could along the underside of his cock. He could feel it the most when his medial ring dragged back and forth over Damon's tongue, yet Logan did not have the restraint necessary to pull back enough to slide his flare over that devious appendage too. As much as he enjoyed just how Damon would adore and please his flare, dragging his tongue around, circling it, dipping it into the slit right on the flatter top…

"Unff…"

Logan panted heavily, warming up, his short coat of hair darkening a little, only mildly, in patches of sweat. Unlike some other anthros, horses were able to sweat from every part of their body, which helped them release heat even while it did sometimes render them a little muskier than others. At least it was easy enough to shower off, so it wasn't something that usually bothered them, even as a richer, more earthen scent that was not of the land around them drifted on the air.

Inhaling deeply, Logan let out a long, drawn-out groan.

"Nnngghhh…"

He felt rather than saw Damon chuckle around his cock. That damn colt liked to know when he was getting to him, though Logan wasn't going to spare a moment to roll his eyes. Not as he slid his fingers into the increasingly messy drape of Damon's mane and clenched his fist hard – but not hard enough that Damon would do anything more than grunt around his cock. They knew their limits and Damon had a safe word too if he ever needed to stop for any reason at all, one that worked when his mouth was full also.

So, they were fine. Fine to enjoy the moment, the contrasting music of birdsong in the trees layering around them. The rest of the world moved right on by without knowing or caring what they were up to, Logan holding Damon's head still as he plundered his sweet, hot mouth.

"Unff… You know just what…you fucking do to me," Logan panted, pausing for breath where he should not have needed to. "Mmm… There's nothing like your mouth."

Damon whined, head spinning pleasantly. He couldn't help himself from dropping a hand to his cock, curling his fingers desperately around it. Of course, he wanted Logan to be the one to get him off, though Logan made that more and more difficult with every passing second, Damon's hips trying to pump helplessly, need curling and pooling warmly in the pit of his stomach. The pressure on his balls, from his underwear and where his jeans had been pulled down that little bit, was immense, though it was entirely from his own arousal, fire flickering and licking up eagerly at the cavern of his insides.

That need… It could only be sated through one means, one thing and one thing alone.

"Ah-ah-ah, colt," Logan tutted, his tongue clicking against the roof of his mouth to draw Damon's attention. "Are you so riled up that you can't even forgo touching yourself for a few minutes? So naughty…"

Damon whimpered, his hands resting on his thighs, fingers curling around and gripping his quads the best he could. That wasn't fair… And why did being called "naughty" get his cock even harder than before? He thought he was into praise!

Yet the body and the mind were tricky subjects to deal with when it came to sexuality and power play – and the two of them were merely along for the ride at that time while the stallions worked out a little more about what appealed to them personally.

The risk of it all got to them more than expected and Logan groaned as, finally, he dragged his aching cock from Damon's lips. It was harder than it had any right to be (in multiple ways), the flare thick and swollen, almost as if he was on the edge of orgasm. Yet the big draft stallion had more stamina in him than that and he was not going to give up his seed so quickly, no, not even when his cock ached and pulsed in that deviously delightful special way.

"Mmm…"

Damon looked up at him, his big, blue eyes so desperate, so plaintive. Logan's heart skipped a beat. He could have given Damon exactly what he wanted right then and there, though he wanted to take his time, to drag things out just a little more. All to see whether he could make his sweet little pony whinny at a pitch that would have heads turning miles away…

"Up here now," Logan grunted, a gentle note in his tone, regardless of how firm he was being. "Turn around."

Damon followed his instruction, ears twitching where he did not quite understand. All became clear when Logan guided him to place his hands on a thicker tree that stood behind them, though neither horse cared what species the tree was. It was just there to serve a purpose and only that, offering Damon some semblance of stability, the pony leaning into it and blushing hard as he arched his back.

It did not seem like all that long ago at all he had been strutting down the canal path, knowing that Logan was looking at his ass, grumpy at being dragged out on the evening. Did sex count as cardio? He didn't think so, not even as Logan tugged down his jeans with some difficulty, along with his underwear, yet only enough to expose the thick, round doughnut of his tail hole.

"Mmmph…"

"Relax for me…" Logan groaned, licking his lips with a lewder, wetter smack than he had most likely intended. "I know you can take me…"

Damon knew that, though that did not stop a shiver of tantalising trepidation – the best kind – from rippling through him. He whuffled softly, nosing at the bark before him, wondering just how hard he was going to be gripping it in but a few moments. The flat, flared head of his boyfriend's dick teased up at against the velvety underside of his dock as he flagged his tail high, tracing a luscious path down to the tight pucker of his tail hole.

The stallion took a deep breath – but the first penetration would always come with an element of strain to it. There was no pain, but it was close to the line. Still, Damon would never have denied himself that, as long as he was alright and well in his own body and mind, even putting more of an arch into his lower back and dropping his torso so that he could grind back onto Logan's member.

The flare ground its way into him, burrowing deeper and deeper, though it was by no means anywhere it had not gone before. Damon shivered, Logan's fingers tracing a line down his spine, rooting him in the moment and soothing him, even though Damon was more than capable of taking it. Inch after delectable inch disappeared into his backside, stretching his pucker wide, and Damon nickered throatily, his head spinning.

It was all he needed, all he wanted, nodding quickly when Logan asked him if he was okay to continue. Fuck, yes, he wanted to continue, to take the powerful, driving strokes that Logan offered him so readily. Sometimes, they would switch and he would be able to top Logan, but there was no real question about who held the reins between them in the sexual side of their relationship.

"Unff…" Damon moaned, trying to keep his eyes open but mostly failing to. "Please… Yes…"

"Of course, colt," Logan nickered, his tail lifting in a flag and a swish, the hairs lashing the air, if only briefly. "Anything for you."

His fingers curled around Damon's hips, holding him steady, though both equines were so close to the edge already it would not take long at all before they reached their highs. There was, after all, only so much that could be done in that regard, since they had worked each other up and been teased so wonderfully already. It was just the grand finale that both equines ached for, soft grunts and pants breaking their lips with every slow thrust of Logan's hips.

Damon nickered, his cock bobbing before him, still achingly desperate. He didn't usually stay hard, not to that extent, when he was being fucked – something about the pressure inside his anal passage, he'd never really bothered looking much more into it besides knowing it was normal. And yet, that time, his cock was harder than ever, leaking pre-cum with every slow, rolling slam of Logan's cock. Damon swallowed a squeal, wanting to jig a hoof in the air and kick out, though he could not and would not, not when his partner was poised behind him, pleasuring him with that long, thick length of stallion cock.

"Oof… Yes…" He moaned. "More…"

Logan was more than willing to deliver, picking up the pace once he was sure that Damon could take it and thrusting long and hard at a steady pace. Of course, there were some erratic shifts and judders of his hips, the stallion tensing and contracting his glutes when his need rose to such a point that he didn't quite know whether he was going to be able to hold off for long enough or not. Yet it did not truly matter, as long as they both got what they needed, from the moment and each other.

He relaxed into it, sliding his hand down and around to grip Damon's cock, his fingers easily encircling his girth. Damon whinnied, eyes wide, trying to hold back his cries; Logan only smiled.

"Take it all, pony."

Sometimes, words did not have to be eloquent. The moment could be just as it was, for the moment was more than enough. He relished in the tight squeeze of Damon's tail hole with every thrust, determined to claim more from him, though it was the pump of his hand, working up and down the full length of Damon's dick, that did it for the colt in the end. His thrusts almost didn't matter as he teased that hard length, tightening his grip just behind the head as he played with the flare.

"Cum for me, colt."

He was a stallion of few words when he was that close to orgasm himself, yet he'd already caught Damon's fingers gripping the back fervently, with a biting edge of desperation. Yet there was no need for Damon to hold back, not even then, not as Logan thrust and tried to grind up against his prostate the best he could from that angle, rubbing his palm over the smooth length of his cock as the colt let out an ear-splitting whinny. It was much louder, clearly, that Damon had intended, but some things could not be stopped once they had begun, the shrill cry fluttering from his lips and nostrils as he neighed out his orgasm to anyone that cared to hear him.

Long, hot spurts of stallion seed painted the bark before him, Logan roughly able to keep his dick pointing forward away from them, so it at least didn't get on their clothes. That was one walk of shame that neither was going to be all that keen to get wrapped up in! Yet all was well as orgasm rolled through Damon, the fervent, rushed pace of Logan's hips picking up more and more.

While the pony's tail hole tightened divinely around him, he could only keep going, feeding those breathy pants and groans, once his whinny had softened, with deep strokes of his cock. He released Damon's dick as the last spurts were drooling out, his cock tipping down lightly as it mildly softened, powering into him with strong, deep thrusts. Logan panted through flared nostrils, the stallion's ears back and pinned, even though there was not a drop of aggression in him. There never had been.

"Unff… So…close…"

And that was all Logan got out as he groaned, clamping his jaw shut, throaty snorts breaking his silence. The hot, heady puffs filled the air as his flare fully engorged within Damon's tail hole and he kept thrusting and thrusting – through his orgasm, spending even longer, thicker ropes of hot horse cum into his boyfriend's backside. Every drop seeped up where it belonged, flooding Damon's tail hole, his partner quivering against him, practically hugging his chest to the tree in a futile attempt to keep his quivering legs somewhat upright.

Yet Logan didn't want to pull back – and neither did Damon want him to either. The moment was right, just for the two of them, even if they would soon have to clothe themselves again and head back. No one had come by and the only witness to their shared lust had been the local wildlife. And they weren't exactly about to tell any tales.

Huffing hotly, the stallion licked his lips as he leaned over his partner, placing the flat of one hand up against the tree to stabilise himself. His cock stayed deep, slowing his thrusts, taking every last scrap of pleasure he could while he buried his shaft inside the only heat that mattered. There would never be anything or anyone quite like Damon wrapped around his cock, though it would take some kinkier play for them to dig even deeper into that, the tangible play of domination and submission that, so far, had only been dipped into.

Yet not everything had to be explored quickly. They had the rest of their lives together to see just where their passions took them and what they wanted to delve into more in the bedroom. And, sometimes, even outside the bedroom…

In time, they would take on even more together, though the frenzied re-clothing and giggles in the giddy afterglow of orgasm just sealed the deal even further between the stallions. There'd be round after round more lying in wait for them when they got home, though the risk of getting caught and the thrill of doing it outdoors, for a little while, would prove hard to beat.

Damon even thought he may well have been more eager to head out on evening walks and random adventures with his boyfriend… Maybe.

Only the experiences themselves would tell those tales.

Between the Studs

It was not quite how Dylan expected his night to go, down on his knees with three other stallions standing over him, painting his face with their cum, but it certainly wasn't a bad way at all to spend an evening.

Yet how the stallion had got to such a position, beside the outdoor hydrotherapy pool at the spa with the water bubbling pleasantly from the jets, was another question entirely. What had started out as a friendly hang out with friends from the leisure and spa complex he worked at changed everything in a single night.

Dylan was not all that sure about hanging out with them, though the other stallions were liked well enough at his workplace. The leisure and spa complex was designed to be relaxing, often with soft music playing in areas outside the gym, where cardio and weightlifting equipment resided, though no serious lifters or fitness folk would really work out there. It was great for maintaining condition and tone, a certain level of fitness, yet for working on muscle building for guys, well…it was not the place.

But that was okay. Not every place had to suit the needs of all and Dylan had found that he fit in well there, taking care of spa patrons and hosting them so that their stay there was as pleasant as possible. He begrudged, ever so slightly, he was not able to afford the services there for himself but, well, at least he had access to the facilities. That was a very good thing indeed.

Glass windows looked out over the hydrotherapy pool from the hallway where the sauna and steam rooms were, offering separate sections that were both indoors and outdoors for spa patrons to enjoy. Sometimes, Dylan glimpsed himself reflected in those windows, his softly golden coat on show and glossy in his reflection. As a palomino, he typically had a golden, glowing sort of appearance, though he had to keep his man and muzzle, in particular, in good condition to maintain himself for work at the spa.

Andrew, Harley and Leo worked in treatments and the gym, offering specialist massages along with personal training, though he had not quite managed to get along with the stallions at first. That evening, they were the only four left behind, Andrew trotting casually through from the gym with a towel slung around his neck and his chest bare.

"Hey, Dylan," he greeted him with an easy grin. "Didn't think you'd still be on this late, I didn't see anyone in the spa area when I passed."

He smiled, looking up from the check in and out book at the reception desk.

"Yeah, I got lucky today," Dylan answered. "Looks like the last group that was supposed to come tonight had a cancellation. So, I still have to stay to close up and everything, but there's not too much to do until then. I can make sure everything's nice and neat and tidy."

"Hm..." Andrew chuckled, eyeing him up casually. "You're always so efficient... This place runs hell of a lot better since you joined the team, you know."

"Oh!"

Dylan blushed, tilting his muzzle away. He hadn't been expecting that compliment, though he could not have said that there was not a part of him that didn't like being caught off-guard too. He wanted to be more comfortable with compliments, though that was something that was much easier said than done. Andrew smirked covertly, the grey stallion's tail flicking and swishing slowly, hypnotically, against the back of his legs.

"Anyway," Andrew said, moving the conversation on easily when Dylan did not seem to be able to pick it up. "We're going to make use of the facilities this evening and hang out by the pool. Don't worry, we've already arranged to have it mopped afterwards, we're not going to make more work for you."

Dylan smiled.

"Oh, that's great," he said, genuinely glad that the guys were going to use the employee perks. "You can stay past closing, if you like, there's no rush. Tonight, I've got nowhere to be."

"Then you should join us."

"Huh?"

Dylan blinked, drawn up short. The guys, Andrew, Harley and Leo, had never invited him to join them before. Truth be told, he hadn't made it known either that he would like to join them or even said anything about hanging out with them before. He knew it was not on them to do everything, yet it was tricky for the stallion, sometimes, to step forward and make the first move.

Even when it was just regarding friends.

"Yeah, of course," Andrew said, stepping back and gesturing outside, where the pool waited. "We're not going to use the indoor but might head into one of the saunas or the steam room too, if you can't find us. If you've not got work to do, patrons to look after, you should definitely come out."

"Yeah… Okay!" He grinned. "Sure, I can do that. See you in ten?"

"Yep," Andrew said. "Out by the pool."

As the grey stallion left, Dylan's eyes dropped to his muscled backside. He didn't know whether the stallion wore tight shorts just to show it off, but his gym attire, with his chiselled chest bare too, didn't leave much at all to the imagination. Even in the front, there was a bulge at his crotch, betraying the size of his sheath and balls, even when they should have been presentably tucked away for exercise, surely. Dylan wore looser jogging bottoms and a T-shirt for exercising, to be fair, not the sort to wear tightly fitted clothing at all.

His lean form starkly contrasted Andrew's muscle, however – and Harley and Leo were about the same too. Each stallion, the grey, the chestnut and the black, were all different with slightly different body types, but their focus on fitness, health and, of course, muscle was clear. He didn't honestly know how they kept themselves in such good shape using the centre's facilities, but, well, they most likely worked out elsewhere too. They certainly ate enough to feed their bodies.

Still, Dylan didn't know what was going to happen when he grabbed his bag, checked all was in order at the desk and headed into the male changing rooms, his pale white tail swinging lightly behind him. It took him no time at all to change into his comfortable swim trunks, not needing anything more than that to head through to the pool and spa areas from the changing area. If he had been a spa guest, or if it had been busier, it would have been prudent and modest to grab a robe too, though he planned to spend most of his time in the water.

Having a soak, at the very least, would be very much appreciated.

The others were already in the outside pool, which was for sitting and soaking, not swimming, when he got out there, arms spread over the edge so that they could lean back and get comfortable. Ears and heads swivelled in his direction as he headed over, waving his hand weakly in a soft greeting.

"Uh, hey, guys, still okay if I join?"

"Of course!" Harley, a big chestnut with a light muscle gut, snorted, shaking his red brown mane off his neck. "Hop in, the water's great."

The bubbles frothed and churned through the water as he slipped into it, somehow finding himself tucked away between Leo and Andrew as the equines made way for him. He had intended to sit on the end, but, well, sometimes little things like that slipped out of his control.

Leo's thigh brushed his as the black stallion smiled, his eyes half-lidded as he leaned back and groaned comfortably.

"Uhhhh… These jets really are the best."

"Not like a real hot tub though," Harley chimed in. "This one's meant to be comfortable, not hot. Mineral water and stuff."

Dylan chuckled, though didn't feel comfortable enough to add his thoughts on their banter.

"You should know all about this, you know," he teased Harley gently, "being that you work here and all. Dylan could school you on all that the spa covers, couldn't you, Dylan?"

"Uh… Maybe?"

Dylan chanced a grin, sliding down a little more so only his head was above the surface of the water. Maybe he could be a little bolder than he usually was…

"I could probably reel off all the treatments here," he tried, testing the waters, "better than any of you guys who deliver them!"

The horses burst into laughter, so infectious Dylan could not help but chuckle along, glad that his very light brag had landed on receptive ears.

"There you have it then!" Harley crowed, squeezing Dylan's shoulder with his hand and giving him a gentle, playful shake. "You've been here almost as long as us, hot stuff, it's about time we all got to know you properly."

"Yeah, it's been too long," Andrew chimed in, standing slowly and stretching his arms out over his head, bubbles frothing around his waist. "Just going to put some music on."

He drew himself from the pool fluidly, not bothering with the steps, and Dylan's eyes locked onto his backside once again. His swim trunks, when soaked, offered an even better view of his glutes – and his bulge too, once Andrew had turned and flipped on the outside sound system. The wet trunks clung to every curve and nuance of his body as if they were trying to put his body on display, though it was the shape of his sheath and the softness above it that caught Dylan's attention. It was as if the head of his cock was protruding lightly out from his already plump sheath, defining his shaft too, his balls round and full below it.

To his horror, however, as Andrew slid back into the water with soft rock music (a gentle compromise) playing in the background, his body responded. In hindsight, he would wonder how it could not when faced with three very sexy stud stallions, his hard-on rising, slow and fluid, from his sheath and hardening up. He pressed his hands over it, as if that would be enough to shove it back into his sheath, but it was not to be, not as he gasped and swallowed a whinny, his eyes wide and wild with a dangerous rim of white.

"Oh, no…"

"What was that, Dylan?"

Andrew peered at him, the stallion's nostrils fluttering. The bubbles, thankfully, hid the obvious rise of his hard-on tenting out the front of his trunks, though he didn't know how long it would take to go down. It didn't help that Leo was so close to him and, when he tried to scoot away along the underwater bench-seat, he only bumped into Harley instead.

"You okay there?" Harley asked.

Dylan rubbed the back of his neck, leaning back with a blush on his cheeks.

"Yeah, yeah…" He bluffed. "Just been a long day, you know…"

"You really shouldn't work as hard as you do…"

No one would ever find out just where that was going as, at that moment, the bubbles faded. The jets turned off, though the heat in the pool remained at a comfortable temperature, even as the water stilled and, finally, showed what Dylan had been trying to hide.

One thing that had to be said about a horse's hard-on: it was never possible to hide.

Out there, on full display, Dylan froze. His ears slipped back, eyes wide, breath catching in his throat as if a band had suddenly closed around it. Their eyes were all on him, though the horse was not in his right mind enough to know that they were just smirking knowingly, contentedly, at one another. There was not a hint of mockery or disgust in any of them.

Rumbling softly with a nicker, Harley slid his hand up against Dylan's thigh, though the palomino was too quick to flinch away. A gasp broke his lips before he could stop it, strain tensing every tiny muscle in his muzzle.

"Do you like what you see then, cutie?" Harley rumbled, his ears twitching as they pricked, locking onto Dylan. "Didn't think you'd be so eager."

"Um…" Dylan squirmed, heat in his cheeks, clawing its way down his neck, hunching forward to better hide his hard-on. "No… Uh… Sorry, guys, I'm just going to go…"

"Whoa, wait!" Leo flung out his arm, the black stallion's lips twisting in sympathy. "Look, we didn't mean to worry you. We were just teasing. This is all okay, seriously. Actually, we all think you're pretty cute. Wondering if you wanted some fun, you know, while it's all quiet here…"

The black stallion whuffled softly.

"Kinda been wanting to ask you over with us for a while," he admitted. "Probably didn't do it right, hm, yeah. We like you, wanted to have some fun with you. Seeing you get all hot up for Andrew though… Hah, I just wanted to be first!"

"So… Can we?"

Andrew slid in close, resting his hands on the bench on either side of Dylan's thighs. He was lightly trapped, but not in a way that he couldn't get away if he wanted to. The choice, ultimately, was still his.

And the grey stallion was so close to him, his arms sculpted and defined in a way that, even then, made him ache desperately to slide his hands down them. A lustful part of him longed to memorise every part of the stallion's body – and the others too. And they liked *him*!

Vaguely, Dylan's ears twitched at the notion of doing anything out there in the open, at the spa – yet the thought was swiftly chased away again.

"I think…" His hard-on really should have spoken for him, licking his lips to moisten his mouth a little. "Yeah… Yeah, I'd like that…"

"Mmm… Then we'll see what you like, cutie."

He liked being called that too, amazed that the three ripped studs liked his slim form enough to tease him out there. Yet there was not all that much time at all for Dylan to wonder at how things had come to pass, not as Leo came in close, all three stallions trapping him playfully in against the side of the hydrotherapy pool.

With them blocking his way, he could languish there as Andrew slid his trunks down slowly, pinging them off the trembling head of his shaft. The flat tip begged for attention and Andrew's hand closed around it quickly, claiming it as his own. There was nothing, however, that the bigger equine needed to do to get Dylan hard and ready.

"Fuck, Dylan, you're so eager," Andrew hissed out through his teeth, the hint of a whicker in the back of his throat. "Fucking love it…"

Dylan didn't know what to think. So, it was a good thing indeed that an overdose of pleasure made it hard to think and easier to be there, relaxing into the moment and only that. Frankly, what did he even have to worry about?

It was not what he had expected of the evening and he leaned back, whimpering softly in the back of his throat as Andrew teased his cock, sliding his hand from the base to the tip and back down again. The skin tried to tug along with the pull of his hand as he masturbated Dylan, yet the horse's cock was too firm to give up quite yet. The flare throbbed, Dylan gasping shortly, though the equine didn't know what to do, not at all, overwhelmed with desire.

"Ah… Fuck…"

"Don't worry, I've got you…" Andrew murmured, the stallions more intent on taking care of the more submissive member of their group than taking advantage of him. "Hm… Have you taken a cock under your tail before?"

Dylan whimpered, another hand roaming around his thighs, spreading them, while another squeezed under his buttocks. He flinched and grunted as a finger quested all the way around and under him, teasing the pucker of his tail hole.

"Ah… Oh… Yeah, yeah, of course…"

He meant that too, though he doubted very much he had taken something or someone as large as the stallions inside him before. As long as they were slow, at least to start, everything would be okay though. He really didn't have anything to worry about.

Just pleasure. Insidious, teasing, delightful pleasure as Andrew helped him out of his trunks and the rest of the horses made sure to get rid of theirs too. They were not needed, no, not when their cocks were rising and treating Dylan to a most intoxicating, invigorating sight indeed.

Three throbbing stallion cocks. His mouth watered, even as Andrew guided him up, checking in with him the whole time, on to the edge of the pool, water streaming from his body. He laid back, though they were still there, ingrained in his mind.

Andrew's dick was long and grey, mottled with a few, very faint, spots of pink. The flare already appeared soft and spongy, so much so that he already ached to take it into his mouth, tonguing and caressing that cock tip. Harley, on the other hand, didn't have a spot of pink on his cock, a darker shade of grey that was much closer to black, though the base below the medial ring seemed much thicker than that of the others. Finally, there was Leo, the black stallion's cock surprisingly light in shade, more pink than it was grey, the darker spots mottling after the medial ring, closer to the base. Each one was unique, though Dylan's pink length begged attention as the grey stallion whuffled softly and lined up his lightly pulsing prick with his tight tail hole.

Dylan relaxed as Andrew leaned over him, bearing his legs back so that his bent knees pushed back closer towards his chest. It was easy, however, for the heat of the stallion against him simply made him want to relax, easing soft inch after inch of that delicious cock inside his backside.

"Ohhhhhh…"

"Easy, colt…"

Fuck, that was hot too. Much hotter than it had any right to be, though Dylan was along for the ride anyway. He was there to take everything the trio had for him, even as Leo took charge of massaging his cock, squeezing his fingers lightly around it as he worked up and down Dylan's length, ensuring that the palomino's pleasure didn't get forgotten about. Not that Dylan needed even more stimulation than he was already getting, his backside so wonderfully full of stallion cock.

"Ohhh, harder…"

"Heh…" Andrew smirked above him, dipping his muzzle, though Dylan's legs were not quite flexible enough to bend back much further, closing the distance between them. "You're needy… I didn't think we'd get inside you this quickly. Unff… Hell, we were going to let you at us first!"

Dylan moaned and blushed, squeezing his tail hole around the massive prick spearing him open. Why were they asking him to talk when all he wanted to do was to soak in just how good it felt to be fucked?

"I… Mmm…" He groaned. "I… I don't really…top…"

"Fine by us…"

Leo squeezed his dick, rubbing his thumb over the flare, though Dylan tensed sharply, not yet ready to cum. He wanted to hold off for longer, to relax into the moment, to keep his hold on the moment and savour everything that he was being given. He wasn't all that much of an active player, not with the water lapping softly on the edge of the pool, the stallions crowding him, but as long as everyone was engaged that was really not an issue at all.

Harley scrambled up out of the pool, kneeling behind his head. The position was odd, too close, the stallion blocking out the outside lights that cast a favourable, soft light over them out there. It leant the hydrotherapy pool an intimate air, as if they were all coming together somewhere more private than they actually were. The horse's cock bopped him on the nose and Dylan grunted, looking up at Harley while the chestnut tried to position himself a little more comfortably.

"Unff, this is going to be a funny fucking angle…" Harley groaned. "Ah, to hell with it… Tap out if you need to anytime, Dylan, we got you."

Only when Dylan opened his mouth did he feed his cock inside, the horse gulping him down with his head laid back all the way onto the smooth, warm stone. Dylan didn't know whether the stone was warm from his body or the pool, but it really didn't matter, not as he was treated to the sensation of hot, smooth horse cock grinding into his mouth. His tongue teased over the flare as he did his best to lap, but it was the kind of mouth fucking where he was more of a passive player, a hole to be filled while he swam in ever so sweet submission.

With a cock in his mouth and one in his ass, there really was nowhere else that he would have rather been. There was a world of opportunities before him with the trio, yet he needed to get to know them on an intimate, personal level too.

Having fun, however, took precedence that night. He gulped around the cock in his mouth, drooling from the corners of his lips, eyes half closed. They didn't need to be open, not when he relished and drank down every sensation, comfortable and content exactly where he was.

Maybe that was the kind of spa day he wanted, really. But Dylan wasn't really thinking, not as Leo's hand squeezed at the base of his cock, pressing his sheath back a little more, exposing a sliver of his cock that he swore had never been out in the open before. The sensations, all crowding in on one another, were too great, though not even the hardness of the stone pressing up under his back was enough to stave off his deep arousal.

No... It was not comfortable and yet that made it even more real. It was rough and it was raw, especially as Andrew sped up, thrusting harder and faster, egged on by Dylan, the stallion grasping his hand. Dylan needed that to root him in the moment, linking his fingers with Andrew's, though he wasn't thinking of tapping out and telling them to stop, to go slower, not at all.

He was happy there, just wanting to drag it all out, to enjoy everything to the very best of his ability, as if it was a dream that could be ripped away from him at a moment's notice.

Yet it was real, very real, as his pleasure mounted more and more. The trio didn't cum yet, however, though Leo was not having his cock tended to in any way, Dylan drooling around the fat length in his mouth. He moaned, not really present in his own reality, though he was more than ready to take the heady thrusts from Andrew, the grey stud's hips bouncing off the backs of his thighs with every powerful stroke.

"Unff... Nnghhh..." He groaned, powering into Dylan as if there could be nothing else in his mind at all, his entire attention on Dylan. "Cum for us...little pony."

Dylan whinnied, long and loud, his shrill cry bouncing off the glass walls that enclosed the pool area, the open sky above him. His cock jerked and flexed in Leo's hold, sending off thick spurts of cum over his golden belly. He couldn't stop and neither did he want to stop as he painted his own palomino coat with his seed, pleasure overwhelming, clenching down around Andrew's cock in his ass. The tightness was too much, the sense of being stuffed full too potent for even his mind.

He relaxed back, Harley withdrawing from his muzzle, though Dylan grumbled and reached for him, wanting that cock back. Why had they taken the dick away from him? That wasn't fair!

But the stallions were merely letting him ride out his orgasm and taking care of him too, sliding him up on to the stone paving around the pool. Andrew's rock-hard shaft slid from his tail hole, leaving the pucker crudely gaping, but Dylan had no concern at all about that. He would tighten up again soon, no matter what pornos tried to make stretched holes look like. He wouldn't even have minded really pushing his limits and seeing just how much he could stuff up under his tail.

One day. Just… Just not that day. Not with his senses returning to the solidity of his reality, being sat up on one of the loungers and a straw pressed to his lips. Dylan chuckled and tried to say that he didn't need a drink, though he was actually rather thirsty.

"Mmm…"

He grumbled around the straw and drank his fill. It helped, at least, feeling a little more refreshed, despite the loose, soft tiredness lining his limbs. He was not done yet though, not with three hard cocks being presented to him, the stallions still hard and Harley's still damp, somewhat, with the faintest smear of his saliva. Andrew took a moment to wash off his shaft and Dylan's stomach lurched with the implications of what that could mean. It could only be good.

"You're not going to go without your turn too, are you?" He all but purred, sliding to his knees and addressing all three of them at once. "It would be a shame to waste these…"

He highlighted what he meant by stroking each of their cocks in turn, hefting them in his hands, rubbing and teasing, sliding his fingers up and around the flares where the glands were the most sensitive. Andrew grunted, probably the closest to the edge of all of them already, though Dylan's cock wanted to harden up again too.

He would just need a little time to get ready for the "more" that he knew, without really knowing, was coming. His lust was still up and he put on his best coy smile (it didn't really work when he was down on his knees) as he gazed up at the stallions, inviting them all to do with him as they willed.

Andrew, with his chiselled, muscled form.

Harley, the heavy lifter with a muscle gut.

And Leo, a little softer around but with a comfortable sort of form: fit and yet the sort that could be snuggled into.

Okay, so maybe he could have let Leo take him first. But there would be time enough for that as he took Leo's cock instead, reverently, into his mouth, sealing his lips around it and suckling softly.

"Ah, fuck… Your mouth…"

It was good to be able to get Leo to make those soft little grunts, the stallion rolling his hips and thrusting lightly as if he didn't want to be too rough with Dylan. Dylan moaned around his length, losing himself there, for he already had all that he needed there to root him where he belonged.

He could languish right there, the soft bubble of the pool in the background, the music lifting a little, playing through a mild rock ballad. The soft lighting cast tantalising shadows over the stone, hinting at what was hidden and what could be revealed, yet their reflections glanced off the windows, highlighting the debauchery taking place in what should have been a place of calm and serenity.

The stallions took their own form of calm as Dylan ignored the stone bearing up against his knees and swapped between their cocks, wanting to taste each one. Harley had the thickest flare of all, throbbing faintly as if he was about to pop off, though Dylan carefully worked them all up, as his own cock hardened once more, so they were close to the edge together. Playing them back and forth from that edge was the best thing of all, hearing them grunt and snort – yet they all allowed him to toy with their cocks as he willed. Despite Dylan being on the bottom, he still had agency and control over what he did.

Maybe this all could be even more fun…

He'd see that in time. Leo thrust, winding his fingers almost tenderly into Dylan's white mane, grinding his cock into his throat. Lacking a gag reflex, all Dylan had to do was keep his head still, letting Leo do as he willed with him. He tongued the underside of his cock as if worshipping him, hands on the stallion's thighs until they slipped around to the inside, groping and weighting his balls in his hands just to feel how much cum was inside.

He was going to get the cum shot of his life, that much was sure!

The stallions, however, had to pull back eventually, letting Dylan moan and lap at their cocks, swapping between them all in such a state of lust that it was as if, once again, he was overwhelmed by choice. Dylan panted heavily, huffing out breath through flared nostrils, eyes flicking from one to the other, their hands working their cocks over furiously with only one intent in mind.

"Mmm… Yes… He moaned, groping his own hard shaft, teasing the flare. "Yes… Cover me…"

Leo climaxed first, neighing out loudly and stomping as a thick jet of cum arced beautifully over Dylan's muzzle. It splattered over his snout and between his eyes, though Dylan was quick to close his eyes to make sure that nothing got where it was not supposed to go. All he could do was relinquish control to the stud stallions, another jet of cum hitting him from Harley and then, finally, Andrew coming after that, as if the visual stimulus had been simply too much for him to hold back from.

He took it all, every splattering spurt of cum painting his muzzle, filling his mouth as he let his jaw hang slack, tongue pressing out slightly over his lower lip. He was just there as a vessel in that moment, something that they could use to get off on – and he loved it exactly how it was.

"Ah… Mm…"

Dylan gulped, swallowing what he could, not wanting to let their seed go to waste as he licked his lips and strings of it drooled over him. Yet the facial, as divine as it was in a location that, really, none of them should have been fucking in, was not the end. No, for the stallions would get him all cleaned up again for more fun elsewhere in the spa, until Dylan came to learn that that was just what happened there after hours. After all, none of them were dainty and delicate and feeling so good with hands roaming over them, massages giving and coat treatments supplied, came with the "price" of needing to spend that lust in other ways.

To be filled and to be taken… There was nothing better Dylan could have anticipated. Though it was Leo, ultimately, who he had eyes for.

The days and weeks and months to come would show just what lay in store for them, growing closer and closer, something burning more deeply than any of them could have imagined – not just Dylan! But they wouldn't stop fucking Andrew and Harley, regardless.

Not when their passion was to be shared.

Claimed by the Water Horse

Puffing clouds of frozen breath like a steam engine, Damien hitched his backpack up over his shoulder blades, groaning as the weight of it hung heavy on his back. Riddled with holes, it was a pack that he simply wasn't willing to give up and his hike that day was one more adventure in the long life it had led and was continuing to lead. Pausing on a ridge, he dropped to a knee, wincing at the freezing wind that made him wish that he'd brought a scarf along. He had not thought it had been so cold. He cursed, rubbing his hands together, gloved yet still chilled to the bone, and berated himself for thinking he knew better, once again, one curse rolling into the next.

He rubbed the back of his hand across the bristle on his chin, checking the map clutched in his other hand with such a fixed grip that one would have thought it was a lifeline. And, in all honesty, it should have been. It should have been more than enough to allow him to find his way across the mountains – it should not have been a long hike at all, just a short one while he found his hiking feet again.

Yet that was not the case.

He squinted at the map, turning it upside down as if that would better allow him to find his bearings in the wilderness. Lines squiggled together into a blur of terrain changes and landmarks that had once been there but had since been claimed by the terror of erosion and climate change. He shook his head and screwed up the map, shoving it back into his pocket, a crumpled mess of once fine paper. Maybe it had been accurate twenty, maybe thirty, years ago, a stolen find from his father's hiking equipment. Its accuracy in current times, with global temperatures rising and weather affecting the landscape even in the wilderness of the United Kingdom, was mediocre at best.

"I'm lost," he said aloud, voice childlike and small in the open air. "I'm actually lost."

Damien scoffed at himself, dry lips twisting to contort his otherwise handsome face into an expression of derision. Rolling his eyes, he threw his hands up to the sky.

"For fuck's sake..." He slammed a booted foot into the ground and snarled at nothing at all, teeth bared like an animal. "This could only fucking happen to me, couldn't it?"

He stormed in a circle, kicking up loose stones as the ridge sloped sharply down and down and down into a dark, bitter valley to his right, ignorant as to the risk of his situation. He could tumble down there with one slip of his foot and, well, who would find him then? He'd be just as lost and gone as the rest of the sorry buggers that disappeared into the mountains never to return. Shaking his head, he forced himself to be still, palms pressed together in the imitation of prayer that would not come to his lips. How could he have thought everything would be the same, that it would be as easy as before?

Muttering incoherently, his growls and grumbles blended into one long stream of abject discontent. Just what the hell was he supposed to do, out there in the middle of nowhere? How long had he been walking for? He checked his watch, lips pursed. Eleven. So that made it...what...five hours? He laughed aloud, though there was no humour in the sound. What had possessed him to get up at such an ungodly hour? How could he have ever thought it would be a nice, easy hike?

Dragging the map from his pocket, he peered at it as if finding it difficult to read, eyes narrowed. Although the basics of the terrain were somewhat similar – in an edited novel kind of way, separating the end result from the initial, unpolished draft – the slopes were steeper and the peaks increasingly jagged the further he traipsed from humanity. He sighed, shoulders slumping. He didn't even know what direction civilisation was in anymore.

So much for getting away from the daily grind and the problems of real life, he thought, quieting his grumbles the best he could. *Can only try to get myself out of this sodding mess now...*

He pushed up on to his tiptoes and peered down into the valley, the bottom shrouded in gloom.

But which way?

Everything looked the same. Setting his shoulders, he held the map before him like a talisman and strode along the ridge, letting himself take in the scenery. If it was all going to pot, he may as well enjoy the view on the way down, he reasoned wryly with himself, dark humour returning with a gleeful flicker of mirth. It shouldn't have been funny, the fact that he was lost with little to no idea where on earth he was, but it was – it absolutely was.

A wild giggle broke his lips and he shook his head over and over again, eyes sweeping the rolling mountains that cut into the sky as if they were trying to split the very fabric of the atmosphere in two. The thing that struck him about the landscape, in stark contrast to the browning foothills and dank grey of the city, was the *green*. If there was one thing he'd take away from the experience – if he survived, that was – it would be all the *green*. Wherever he looked, luscious grass took hold, cropped close to the ground around rocky outcrops by the elements, yet it was still irrefutably fresh and damp underfoot.

They didn't have green like that down on the flats anymore. Farmland was fed by a synthetic brand of shrub that suited domesticated farm animals and growing crops alike, leaving everything the same shade of beige. The cities tried to make life a little more colourful, perhaps for the simple sake of brightening up the world, although he had his doubts about that, but had, as always, fallen woefully short, colour scripted into man-made atrocities.

But the mountains... He sucked in a breath, even enjoying how the icy air burned his lungs. The mountains were untamed. They stood through all the horrors committed to the world, even as their landscape was altered, day by day and week by week. Although they would never again be the same with the world shifting around them, he couldn't ever see them falling short of the natural splendour they had always boasted for him and, sometimes he thought, him alone.

He smiled, anger slipping away like water down a creek. That was why he had missed hiking so much. That moment. That moment of peace.

Tension unknotted from between his shoulder blades and he laughed, spinning in a circle with his hands, this time, thrust up to the heavens in joyous admiration of the beauty whatever god was out there had created. As he walked, he struggled to comprehend the scope of daring stretching out in all directions as far as the eye could see – or at least until the mountains cut off anything further from view. But that was okay. He had plenty to admire in the meantime, including a small tarn (a feature of the landscape) cupped in the arms of the mountain, regardless of how badly the day had gone. It couldn't be any worse than living in the city dread: dying in beauty.

As morbid as his humour was, however, he held on to hope that he would find his way out of the mountains or at least back the way he'd come by nightfall. He sighed and pressed his lips together. What now? He couldn't keep walking aimlessly, as wonderful as the scenery was, that much he was certain of.

Casting his eyes back to the little lake, left behind, supposedly, when a glacier melted, he raised an eyebrow. Well, if he had to make a decision, water would be as good a start as any. Who knew if he'd find another fresh store of it for a while?

He gulped, eyeing the slope down to the tarn with trepidation in his eyes, every inch of it covered in loose rock that looked set to shift and tumble as soon as pressure was put upon it. It had probably been left behind when the glacier retreated – a natural inconvenience to the traveller. How much tread was left on the underside of his boots? They were old, one with a hole in the toe that let in water if he was idiotic enough to step into a puddle. Damien steadied himself, checking the straps of his backpack with shaking fingers: too loose, too old, but it would have to do.

Taking each step down the treacherous slope with great care, Damien held his breath as rocks shifted beneath his feet, threatening to send him crashing to the bottom, a broken heap of a man. His heart pounded in his throat, breath raking through his windpipe, and he swore and yelled as he missed his footing, crashing on to one knee. Pain shot up his leg and he rolled his head, grinding his teeth as he struggled to contain the pain. It wouldn't have been manly to shout, even if there was no one out there to hear of his weakness.

Holding his knee close to his chest, he dragged himself up again, eyes watering. It wasn't so bad, it couldn't be so bad, he strove to convince himself, a dull throbbing pain lancing through his entire leg. Not broken, but bloody close. Dabbing at his lip, he winced at the spot of blood staining his glove. He didn't even remember catching it with his teeth when he'd fallen. And he wasn't even halfway down the decline. He almost wished someone would hear his weak, squalling cries, as pitiful as a chick crying in the nest for its mother. Yet no help was forthcoming.

At least from the land.

Slowly, step by step, Damien made his way down to the tarn with only minor further incidents, breath stuck in his throat. Loose rock ground and slid over one another like the plates of the earth as he muttered and swore, relieving the pain in his leg the best he could with curse after curse. Some said swearing helped relieve pain and he wasn't about to contest their logic out in the wilds. Nevertheless, he exhaled a lungful of breath he had not realised he'd been holding as he reached the bottom, legs trembling under the weight of his own body.

He refused to think of how he was going to get home when he could barely put weight on his right leg, however.

Limping to the lake, he missed his footing more than once, wincing as he jerked and jostled his injured leg. The pain didn't seem to be getting any better, but he tried not to think of that as he lowered himself cautiously to the pebbles, worn smooth by the elements, at the edge of the lake itself. He dropped his bag heavily beside him and dug out the empty flask he'd brought in case he needed water, commending himself briefly for remembering to bring that at the very least.

Tipping out the few drops of water remaining – he shouldn't have chugged it so quickly – he pushed it beneath the surface of the lake, rinsing it out and then waiting for it to fill. His lips pursed into a whistle without conscious thought and he sat back on his heels, able to forget his injury for a brief moment. Nothing mattered besides the task at hand and he committed himself to that and that alone.

Until something slithered beneath the surface of the lake, drawing his eye to a dark shape that seemed to duck into the depths, disappearing from view. He blinked, pausing with the flask submerged in the water, bubbles rising to the surface. Swallowing hard, he held firm, refusing to take a step away from the suddenly daunting pool.

A cloud, he tried to reason with himself, laughing shakily. *A cloud. It was just a cloud passing over the lake, a shadow. There wouldn't be anything out here, you bloody know that, come on. Get your head together.*

He let the last glugs of water fill the flask and yanked it from the water, cramming on the top as his heart traitorously hammered, loathing his own tickle of fear. What was he scared of? There wasn't anything there, not really. Just a trick of his eyes, his imagination getting the better of him, just like it always did.

Bubbles floated to the surface and he stumbled back with his mouth agape as a head emerged from the pool, two dark eyes blinking serenely up at him. Two ears, curved like unfurling petals, twitched from side to side, a long jaw stretching down from a dished, shapely cheek down to two flared nostrils. The creature snorted, a plume of water shooting from its nostrils, and spun about, a grey tail not all that far from a dolphin's tail fluke slapping the surface of the lake.

Damien gawped after it like a fool, eyes bulging out of their sockets.

This couldn't be happening, he thought, head whirling, one chasing the other too quickly for him to catch any single one. It just couldn't be... Creatures like that...

He didn't finish the thought, frozen on his backside with his palms splayed flat on the ground beside his hips. As if curious (or perhaps merely hungry), the creature returned, a horse-like head breaking the surface in a spray of cool water. It turned its head from side to side, looking at him with both large eyes, and he held his breath, wondering if it was sizing him up to be eaten.

Far from lunging for him – whether the creature could move on land or not was another question entirely – the animal studied him as scrupulously as he was observing it, each taking in the measure of the other as if they posed an equal threat to each other. The curve of its tail floated to the surface, the tip forming that shapely fluke indeed like that of a marine mammal, and lifted from the water, skin streaming. Damien watched, afraid to move, as the creature waved it gently back and forth, eyes bright as its nostrils quivered in a whinny, burbling with its lips half-submerged.

He started, eyebrows shooting up. Was the animal...saying hello?

Easing on to his hands and knees, he crept closer to the edge of the water, fear trickling away. He reached out his hand, movements tediously slow, as if to touch the flat of its muzzle, coat darkened to stormy grey under its wet cling. The creature – whatever it was – huffed and shot back in the water, dipping below the surface as it sank down and down and down. Scrambling along the shoreline to where a small overhang cut over a drop of darker water, rather than the shallows, he searched for the animal, scanning the tarn repeatedly for a shape that proved elusive when it wanted to be.

"What are you?" He breathed, leaning over the water. "And *where* are you? Come on now..." He squinted. "Come back... I ain't gonna hurt you, don't worry."

He spoke in a low, soothing tone as if the creature would understand the meaning of his words. His reflection danced brokenly before his eyes as the lake rippled, coming back to a juddering representation of his rough features, brown eyes creased with worry at the corners. Damien swept his hand through it impatiently, swiping away the brief glimpse of his brown hair, tousled and dropping into his eyes again, trying to look past it, deeper and deeper into the lake.

As if as curious about him as he was about it, the creature popped its head out and squealed, weaving back and forth in the water as bubbles churned around its arched neck. It struck out with two forelegs tipped with several long spines that boasted slick skin stretched between them – a type of fin, he assumed – and whinnied at such a pitch that he winced and struggled to not clap his hands over his ears. The creature had no hind legs to speak of, now that he could see it at such close quarters, but the aquatic mammalian tail slapped the water, sending up a spray of droplets in a glistening shower.

Damien chuckled, running his fingers back through his hair as the animal bobbed its head. Was it trying to play with him? It thrashed and squealed, flipping over on to its back to complete a perfect loop underwater, only to break the surface again, wet mane clinging to its neck.

"Either I'm hallucinating or you're something very different to anything we've ever heard of or seen in our lands, little fella," he murmured, a smile stretching his lips wide. "Or something we did not think was real at all."

For there was one animal – a myth – that the creature resembled too closely, something from a country far away where mythology was a far more accepted phenomena than what could be found in the

Western world. A creature with a head of a horse and tail of a fish, or close enough, could only be called a hippocampus. He shook his head. Or, to use a term that moved more fluidly over the tongue, a water horse.

"A water horse," he said, fingers outstretched to the creature. "That's what you are. A water horse. A hippocampus. A monster of the deeps and of the lakes from a time that never happened."

The equine eyed his fingers, remaining still as he inched closer.

Perhaps I am something more than what you claim to know, human.

A shriek tore itself from Damien's lips before he could stop it and he shot back, wide eyed and falling over himself in his effort to suddenly put himself as far away from the water as possible. His leg screamed and he swore as it buckled beneath him, sending his body – too heavy for his liking – crashing to the stone with a sickening thud. He rolled on to his back, expecting to find the water horse already in hot pursuit, yet found no body sliding wetly over the stones.

Cautiously, he pushed his torso up from the ground, ignoring the pulsing in his leg the best he could, and braved a look back to the water. The hippocampus bobbed serenely, flicking one ear towards him, only the top side of its muzzle protruding from the water.

Damien pointed a shaking finger at it, working his lips to force out the words that suddenly simply did not want to come.

"You talked."

The hippocampus threw its head up, neck rising, streaming with water.

So I did.

"Horses aren't meant to talk..." Damien forced out stupidly, shaking his head as his gaze dropped to the stones. "This can't be happening... It's not real, got to be imagining things."

To him, it seemed the only sane thing to believe, but the water horse shook its head, somehow managing to appear affronted even without possessing the facial muscles to form humanlike expressions.

I am hardly a horse or an object... Not an "it." The creature snorted. *I am a male. Water horse, if you please. It seems to be all you can get your tongue around.*

He stared.

"You're male?"

If you must assign a sex to me, yes. Yes, I am male.

"And... How are you talking?"

The water horse flicked his tail, slapping the flat side down on the water to make a crack that would have scared any fish away for miles.

Does that really matter? You've already decided I am a creature that does not belong in your world and time. What difference does it make to you whether I can talk or not?

Damien scowled.

"It makes the difference between sanity and insanity, I'll tell you that. You're talking in my mind, aren't you?"

Do you see my lips moving?

The horse bobbed his head, upper lip flapping. Damien stiffened. Was the animal mocking him?

"Not in any sense of speech, no," he muttered. "So why are you here then?"

I could ask why you are invading my territory all the same.

Damien flinched.

"I was exploring! Hiking!" He defended himself, palms facing out in as placating a manner as he could manage. "Is that such a crime?"

The water horse squealed and reared from the water, front fins flashing in the grey light.

Exploring, you say? Yet, you are here and you are lost, human.

He scowled and pushed himself to his feet, doing his best to keep the flicker of pain from passing over his face. Although his leg throbbed something fierce, it could bear some weight – hopefully enough to get him back to safety. And away from a disrespectful hippocampus.

"This has been lovely, chatting with myself in the middle of nowhere," he rattled off, hitching his backpack over his shoulder, "but I really must be off now. I'm lost, as you said, and it's time for me to become very un-lost, thank you very much."

He stumbled over his own feet, ruining the dramatic effect somewhat, and muttered under his breath. The water horse slapped his tail into the water, recalling his attention even as he tried to pad off with what little remained of his dignity. After all, what he was seeing wasn't real and all he was really doing was having a conversation with himself. He didn't think it was possible to go mad in the mountains after only half a day though.

I can help you find your way home.

He stopped in his tracks, looking back over his shoulder.

"What?"

The water horse reared up in the water, throwing his head back so that water spilled off his long, luxurious mane, which must have rippled beneath the surface of the water like kelp.

I can help you find your way home. It's not really all that difficult a concept to understand, is it?

"With an attitude like that, it may well be," Damien grumbled. "So which way is home for me? I started off at the visitor centre."

No one comes from there anymore, he commented. *It's deserted. Where did you really come from?*

Damien rolled his eyes.

"Yeah, well, the map I used was out of date. So, sue me. You can still park down there."

Interesting. I do indeed know where you have come from, if that is the case.

Damien looked expectantly at the water horse, head inclined towards the beast. The equine blinked slowly and yawned, a set of surprisingly sharp teeth flashing. He took a step back.

"Well? Are you going to tell me which way I need to start walking or what? Surely you want me to get the fuck out of here already?"

The water horse surveyed him with what he chanced was a critical eye.

I do not allow travellers to pass on so easily.

Damien started.

"Then what on earth do you want from me?" He spread his hands wide. "I've got nothing for you but the clothes on my back and this bag! It won't be of any bloody interest to you! What use would you have for a few random bits of hiking kit anyway?"

Shaking his head, the water horse swam to the edge of the water where a smooth plane of rock sloped below its surface. Beaching himself like Damien had seen killer whales do on the television – his one vice, he would have told anyone who cared to listen – he slithered on to his side, showing off his gleaming body in all its glory. He stretched out on his side, head pulled up from the stone, and neighed loudly, flicking up his tail in a bold arch. Where his hindquarters should have been, his grey coat gave way to a slippery tail, shining with moisture, curling powerfully against the stone. Damien gulped. One hit from something like that and he'd be out stone cold.

Assist me in release and I will guide you home, human, he whispered, pushing words unbidden into Damien's mind.

Damien bristled, heart hammering. Couldn't he keep the damn beast out of his head? Spoken words were easy enough to block out, but, with how the beast spoke, he heard his words as clearly as if they were his own thoughts. They probably were his own thoughts, he reminded himself.

"I have a name, you know," he snapped. "Why do you keep calling me *human*? Surely you're intelligent enough to understand more than that?"

Ears slipping back to his skull, the hippocampus snorted and shook his damp mane off his neck.

You'll have to tell me what that name of yours is before I can use it...human.

He sighed and rolled his eyes, folding his arms across his chest.

"Damien. It's Damien."

A typical Western name.

"And a typical water horse from myth. Everything about you says how you like wordplay, what tricksters you are, whether you're frolicking alongside ships or luring travellers into lakes."

He laughed and shook his head, hands shoved into his pockets.

"Is that what you want from me? To lure me into this lake so you can eat me?"

The hippocampus studied him, dark eyes unblinking.

And why would you think that? He tilted his head to the side, ears twitching. *Is that solely from what you have heard of my kind? I have already told you what I want from you.*

The man frowned, fingers curling and uncurling. His subconscious must be a real bitch to throw riddles like that at him.

"You haven't told me anything?" He growled. "Release? What the hell is that supposed to mean?"

Are you so familiar with the females of your kind that you don't understand a male in need when he is presented to you?

"A male in *need*?" Damien laughed and threw his head back – it was surreal, it really was. "What, are you horny there, mate? A horny horse?"

He bellowed, bending over at the waist and slapping his knee as if he'd come across the greatest joke in the world. Without an ounce of amusement in his glare, the water horse put his ears back all the way, lifted his head and hissed viciously, the sound curling ominously enough through the air between them that Damien swallowed his mirth abruptly.

Is that amusing to you?

"It's only my head that's funny, mate," he muttered. "What are you wanting me to do then, if I'm to play along with this fucking farce? Find you a girlfriend? I'm sure there's a nice mare or two down on one of the farms if you let me know how the fuck to get out of here."

A stallion would do just as well.

"I'd figured you were a bloke, a boy horse, from your voice," Damien said, scratching his chin. "You're a funny sort of water horse mare then."

The equine drew back his head, affronted.

I am no mare!

Damien's brow creased.

"So, why the hell is a stallion okay then? You're a guy...and you're okay with a stallion?"

He shook his head, droplets of water flying from his mane.

We are not as discerning over sex as your species. He threw his head back as if for effect, mane whipping across his neck, a wet slap of hair. *We are beyond you and your kind.*

Damien raised an eyebrow, coming to the only conclusion he could in the situation. It didn't feel like there was any wrong answer anyway in a conversation entirely with himself. He giggled and clapped a hand over his mouth, only lifting it again, eyes wide, to force out two words.

"You're gay?"

Staring at him, the water horse bobbed and blinked slowly, his mental link to Damien wavering. Damien wiped away tears and snorted into his palm, trying to keep images of a gay horse out of his head. Shouldn't a gay horse be a unicorn? Wouldn't that be more accurate that some weird lake monster? His shoulders shook and he half-turned away as the equine came back to himself, nostrils flaring in a snort.

That would not be the correct term for one of my kind either...

The equine trailed off and shook his head.

It does not matter. It does not seem that you would understand this manner of companionship, though it is of no concern to me. I shall drift on as you remain trapped in a pool of stagnant water, spinning in an eddy until your dying day.

Damien gulped, suddenly sombre at the thought of passing. What was wrong with his head to bring such dark thoughts to the forefront of his mind? Yet the equine pressed on, disregarding his preference to leave the conversation dead in the water, as it were, if it was going to go down avenues like *that*.

It is not what I meant, regardless, that I have a male preference. I only meant to imply that there are swifter ways to find release than to acquire a mate.

Blinking, Damien shrugged and held up his hands.

"There are? How are you going to get off without a bloody girl or boy then? What do you think you're going to do? Or what do you want me to do, if you're going to tell me how the hell to get out of here?"

Eyeing him, the water horse rolled his head down to the stone and waved his tail gently.

I'm confident you will be able to play the part of the mare well enough for me.

Damien stared, words snapping to his lips before his mind truly had a chance to catch up with what the horse had just come out with.

"I'm no fucking girl, mate!"

Snorting, the equine rolled his eyes, splaying his fins out across the stone.

They all say that and yet they all come around to my way of thinking. Sooner or later, that is.

He paused and twitched his ear.

I would much rather you come around to my way of thinking sooner this time, human. It has been far too long since I felt the touch of true companionship.

Scowling, Damien shrugged and held up his hands.

"Sorry, there," he said, though there was not an ounce of sincerity ringing through his tone. "But I can't help you. I'm straight. And you're an animal. Not going to happen."

Do I seem like an animal to you? Do your animals speak as I do?

"Nothing speaks as you do," he muttered. "But can't you just lure, I don't know, another water horse like you into the lake? Or just go find one yourself?" He scratched the back of your head. "Say, you can speak without moving your lips, putting a voice in my head... Well, it isn't a great stretch, now, to think you can somehow get yourself over land too, now, is it?"

Damien stepped back and put his hands on his hips, an absurd smile spreading across his face. He'd gone and done it! He'd outwitted the beast. Or himself. His head spun, swinging between what he thought was real and what he knew was real...or not. He shifted his feet on the stones, peering down as if he suddenly feared they would also shimmer into nothingness, proving the fragility of their scant reality in the moment.

The equine, however, was far from amused by his reasoning. Half-rearing, he heaved himself from the rock and snapped viciously, tail slapping the stone.

I cannot leave my lake, human! He snapped, teeth clicking together sharply as he feigned a lunge, weaving his head back and forth over and over again. *How many times do you believe the elements have carried a partner to my lake? It would be less than any number you could conjure up.*

The man took in a deep breath.

"Wow... So, you've been in there without getting off for, like..." Damien screwed up his face. "Months?"

The equine sighed.

Years would be more accurate. Although not without that simple male pleasure... He squirmed, pushing himself over the stone towards the frozen human. *Other companions have found their way to my lake. Usually male. Never of my kind.*

He paused, eyes bright.

Neither fact matters when it comes to release.

Darren swallowed, comprehension finally grasping his mind and refusing to let go.

"So..." He struggled for words, tongue stuck to the roof of his mouth. "Let me get this straight. Well, no, not straight..."

He winced at the childishness of his own words and tried a second time.

"You want me to get you off...somehow?" He screwed up his face, forehead creasing. "I don't know..."

The water horse lifted his shoulders, set down from his withers, in a shrug, forelegs twitching with the movement. He made as if to wriggle back into the water, tail sweeping back and forth across the ground to propel him forward. Damien almost smiled, despite the offer presented to him: the equine flopped around on land in as ungainly a fashion as a common seal.

Be that as it may, human, if you will not give me what I need. He snorted and shook his head. *But you will not find your way out of the mountains, alive, if you do not help me.*

He bared his teeth.

Perhaps I shall feed on your carcass once you have failed to find your way home? The carrion birds are so wonderful at carrying the choicest morsels to my lake.

The man baulked, eyes wide. His heart hammered against his ribcage and he pressed his hand to it as if he could still its beat. An image of himself lying dead in the mountains, eyes wide and glassy, flashed before his eyes, impossible to disregard. A crow landed on his imaginary corpse and Damien thrust the image from his mind. It didn't belong there.

No. He shuddered away from it and folded his hands in front of his stomach to stop them from shaking. Life was rough, a monotony of the same, but he didn't want to die. That much he could actually be sure of.

So that only left him one option as morning slipped into afternoon. He peered at the sun through the grey clouds half-obscuring it. What time was it even? He glanced at his watch, berating himself for his idiocy in not checking it initially, and a chill ran down his spine. It had stopped at eleven. There was no way to tell how much daylight was left to him before darkness and, judging by the freezing chill in the air, a rolling fog that would hide his still body from sight long before anyone would have the chance to find him in the wilderness.

He took a deep breath, steadying himself as he ran a shaky hand back through his hair. Beads of moisture slipped on to his palm and he stared at the sweat from his forehead as if it was a foreign entity.

"And..." He couldn't believe he was actually considering it. "If I do help you, what happens then?"

The equine turned his head towards him, ears pricked and tail lifted as if eager. Damien licked his lips, still finding it difficult to read the body language of such a strange creature.

You may go on your way and I will direct you back to where you came. He licked his lips, a slender tongue sliding out over a maw that suddenly seemed impossible to ignore, filled with sharp, deadly teeth. *A morsel or two of food for me, if you have something in that pack of yours, would not go amiss either.*

"If you set me on the right path, I'm sure I can spare something for you."

He paused, looking up to the sky as if hoping for divine intervention or, perhaps, sudden inspiration.

"So..." He started, fiddling with his fingers. "How does this go then?"

Come here, human.

"Damien," he muttered even as he slowly traipsed to the water horse's side. "My name is Damien. Get it right."

Inclining his head gracefully, the equine snorted softly.

My deepest apologies. Damien. I require nothing more of you than the touch of your body, however you are able to complete the task.

The man blinked.

"The what now?"

Kneeling, Damien shook his head and cast his eyes down the equine's sleek body, positioned beside his tail.

"Speak English, honestly."

Putting his ears back, the horse blew a wad of watery snot on to his jacket.

That would be language that I'm currently using, human. What I mean is I will allow you to please me using your body in any way that you can. He rested his head on the stone, something shifting against his belly. *That, at least, I will afford you. Do not take my geniality lightly.*

A sarcastic response tickled at Damien's lips, but he bit it back, pushing it down to when he would retell the story to himself at a much later date. Letting his eyes trail reluctantly down the equine's body, he started, seeing something where his coat blended into a tail that had not been there before.

A long, tapered cock with a small, bulging flare at the tip swung, pulled down towards the ground under its own weight. Pinker than a human's shaft, it was raw and animalistic, something that he couldn't imagine was of the world he lived in. But he could hardly think he was falling prey to the pathways of his own addled mind anymore. The cock grew before his eyes, stretching out further and further from a slit in the hippocampus' belly that he had not caught before, so cleverly concealed had it been.

With his cock fully out in the open, the equine seemed to widen his eyes, lifting his tail as if in anticipation or wondering what was taking his temporary companion so long.

Damien tilted his chin up proudly. He just had to not think about what he was doing. He could think he was milking a cow. Wincing, he gnawed the inside of his cheek. That thought wasn't much better, truth be told, but could any thought replace the one of him jacking off a water horse of myth?

Not really.

"Okay," Damien muttered, holding his breath. "Here goes nothing."

Reaching out, he paused halfway through the motion, eyeing the horse distrustfully.

"You better not eat me or something after I've gotten you off, all right?"

The equine inclined his head gracefully.

You have my word. I have already fed on sheep today.

Damien did not know whether that was a good thing or not yet had already committed to the motion. Sliding his fingers around the thicker base of the creature's cock, he flinched from its slimy surface, as if the shaft had been covered in a slick layer of algae. He grumbled to himself, trying to focus on the unpleasantness of the act as he pumped the length, letting his fingers scoot closer together as they rose towards the narrow tip.

As his fingers brushed the tiny flare right at the head, it flexed under his touch, a trickle of what he could only think was thick pre-cum drooling viscously from the head. It caught on his fingers and smeared down the length as he stroked, surprisingly warm as it spread over his skin and the creature's cock.

Sighing, the water horse stretched out as Damien scooted closer, sitting with his backside on the cold pebbles facing the equine's body. He really was a sight to behold, he had to admit, however grudgingly, with a coat shimmering through shades of grey as it dried in the weak, dreary day.

That is wonderful, he murmured, ears drooping softly. *Please continue. Please.*

Damien raised an eyebrow. Was the water horse begging him? It almost sounded like it, yet he did not dare make a comment.

To his shock, he found a flicker of enjoyment in the smooth glide of his hand over the other male's member, easing back and forth with increasing speed and confidence. Every time his fingers rose to the tip, he squeezed just behind the flare, drawing fat spurt after spurt of pre-cum from the shaft as if he was milking it from the source itself. Damien's lips twitched and he adjusted his position as subtly as he could, ignoring the traitorous tightness in his jeans. That could not be right. That was just his clothing shifting uncomfortably. Heat rose across his neck. It had to be.

Refusing to consider any other possibility just at that moment, Damien brought a second hand to the object of his attention, pumping both palms along the length, although he did not need both hands to enclose it completely – he was small enough to handle, at least. Nickering, the equine bobbed his muzzle against the stones, shivering as the wind picked up his drying mane from his neck and played with it in the breeze. Damien grinned, suddenly increasing the pace of his hands, trying to imagine how exactly the water horse would thrust into a partner. It kept him from thinking too much about what he was actually doing if he tried to think about how the beast would mate properly, if left to his own devices.

To his discomfort, however, the imaginings of a water horse twisting sinuously beneath the surface of the water to link his body with a mate – male or female, it did not matter for his mental imaginings – did nothing to ease the tightness in his hiking trousers. The water horse twisted and groaned, stretching out his neck with his ears slipping back as if he was trying to hold back his own pleasure, much like any human male would with a partner.

Close...

The word came faintly to his mind as if the equine was moving away from him, yet he could still feel heat pulsing through his cock, droplets of pre-cum oozing on to his hand. On a whim, he brought one hand to his lips and, with only momentary hesitation, licked off a droplet, lips pursing. It was not an entirely unpleasant taste, sweeter than he had ever heard his semen had ever tasted, but the equine left him no time to ponder further. Lifting his head in a neigh that startled the human almost back to his feet and away, he arched and thrust his own cock between Damien's hands, jerking wildly as his nostrils flared.

There could only be one reason for a male with his cock out to be acting so erratically.

With his whole body convulsing, the water horse squealed and thrashed, tail slapping into Damien's side. Tossed on to his side, Damien landed heavily and swore, pain lancing into his hip. But he couldn't take his hands away from the beast's shaft as it suddenly throbbed visibly in his palms, blood further engorging the fat length as something travelled up a tube suddenly bulging through the underside.

The first rope of seed caught him unaware, shooting across his jacket as he forced himself back to his knees, trying to regain his balance even as the equine twisted through orgasm. His hands slipped and he pumped the shaft the best he could, cum making his position treacherous as it shot out in thick spurts to coat his hands and the underside of the equine's belly, all the way up to his chest. Painting his own grey coat with splashes of white, the equine snorted, tail wriggling back and forth as if with a sudden mind of its own, as the stream slowly tapered off. His cock pulsed one last time in Damien's hands and then was still, though it did not soften in the slightest.

Peace seemed to roll over the dip in the land where the little tarn rested, a weak stream of sunshine breaking through the clouds. The water horse stirred as it cast warmth over his coat, streaked with his own desire.

Now... The water horse rolled his head back against the stones, mane splayed around his ears like a halo. *Now... I shall show you the way back to your home.*

Damien looked down at his hands, splattered with pearly seed, as if he did not know what to do with them. Heat rose to his cheeks, his trousers far, far tighter than they should have been.

Part of him, which he would, of course, never admit to aloud, did not actually want to go. Part of him wanted to stay, to spend more time with the beast and see... Well, he did not know exactly what he wanted to see, only the frantic pounding of his heart told him more than he wanted to hear.

The horse lifted his head, eyes brighter than before. For the first time, he noticed a drop of aquamarine that spread across both orbs, spiralling out like a spider web. He shivered. The creature could not have been from his world — not by far.

But was he real? What was real? Damien set his shoulders back.

Leave... The creature's words flitted weakly, an image of the landscape suddenly thrust into his mind. *You have done your duty. And now you have your way to go home.*

Damien stared, frozen in place with his fingers still slick with cum. The water horse's shaft eased up and back into his sheath without, as far as he could tell by his eye alone, softening at all. He licked his lips, wishing he had the courage to raise his unclean hands – seductively coated – to his lips and taste what he could not conceal he desired.

"But..."

He could not find words to express what he wanted to and the equine pulled his front half up, fins tucking neatly beneath his body.

It is time for you to leave, human. He dipped his head. *Please go onward to the rest of your life.*

Exhausted, Damien stumbled away up and out of the dip of the tarn, a mental map lingering in his mind until his tired feet found the visitor centre and stopped dead. The route he'd taken slipped from memory, fading like a whisper on the breeze, and he looked around the desolate car park and his lone vehicle in the evening gloom, not even remembering how he'd got there. Time had passed without him noticing – or perhaps that was the creature's doing – and he stood at his destination without knowing where to go.

Damien hunched his shoulders. Home. Home was the only place to go. He started the car, warming his hands over the slowly warming air vents as they poured heat into the rickety old car, funnelling it in from the engine. Driving proved to be such a familiar experience that he wondered, surely not for the first time that day, whether he had experienced all he thought he had after all.

Running his fingers over the twist of hair from the water horse's mane much later that night, Damien warmed his toes on the radiator, knowing that, against all odds, he had really met a water horse in the mountains.

The only problem was he wanted to see the hippocampus again, that sleek hide and hard member thrusting themselves unbidden into his mind. Was it a trick of the creature? He had no way of telling as he replayed the memory of stroking the equine's hard cock, hand moving from the base to the tip over and over again as the beast squealed. He blushed, rubbing the back of his neck. Maybe he'd even take his cock into his mouth next time. If he was lucky.

His eyelids drooped.

He hoped he'd be lucky.

Hippocampus' Delight

Did you miss me?

Damien tossed and turned in his narrow little bed, locked into a city flat from which there seemed to be no escape. The sheets tangled and wove around his legs as he muttered and groaned, sweat beading his forehead, but there was no rising from the clutches of a dream that had returned to him over and over again. In his mind, however, he was not in the safety of his own bed but with his head far, far below the surface of the water, darkness swamping him as if it was threatening to drag him right down to the very depths of the underworld itself. A dream, that was all it was, but the very best kind of dream that he wanted to last forever even as he sweated and moaned for a release of an entirely different kind.

And, in that dream, in the dead of the night, resided a water horse, a hippocampus of myth and legend, that flitted and flowed around him, deep in a pool of crystalline water, as if it was soaring through the air itself. He'd only seen the creature once, out in the lakes of mid-Wales when he had strayed from his path, but the memory of his tail, an equine coat blending seamlessly into something mammalian, the hair thinner there, would forever stay with him. But it was only in the realm of dreamland that Damien could entrance himself with the flitting myth of the water horse as he swam back and forth before him, tail flicking gently as if he had every right to be there. He shouldn't have existed and yet…

No… Damien growled to himself, treading water and waving his cupped palms back and forth – sculling, that's what it was called – as the creature circled him. He'd been *there*, he was sure of it. He hadn't imagined anything, simply could not have. That wasn't how things worked, how things were in his own mind. Bubbles streamed from his lips but, somehow, Damien was still able to talk, water pressure bearing down on his ears as he couldn't even see the shimmering skin of the surface anymore.

"Mate, there's something different about you…"

Such eloquence, he really had to commend himself sometimes. Yet was it not true in its essence that there was something different about the hippocampus, something that he had not yet, of course, found in the heart of any human being? Ah, he had not spent much time with him, that much was true, but Damien could not help but shake his head as the creature came to a halt before him, forelegs fanned out so that the fins on his forelegs could spread and aid his stop.

And what draws you to such a conclusion?

Oh, the creature was mischievous, he'd known that from the start, with his slick skin and an equine coat that still seemed to somehow allow the water to run off when he was actually out of the lake. Quite literally, the fur on his body repelled liquid like water off a duck's back, not that Damien would have really have spent all that much time around ducks besides lobbing hunks of stale bread at them in the park.

"A lot…" Damien said thickly, water playing over his lips like the touch of a lover. "You… You're…"

And yet he could not force the words from his lips as his mouth filled with water and he groaned, rolling his head from one shoulder to the other, sinking down and down and down and down. The water horse, of course, followed him but that was just where the dream, each and every time it graced his sleeping mind, changed for a more sultry turn, a twist that no man should have been able to concoct, despite his natural arousal.

For, he'd thought he was a man who liked women – or at least both sexes, equally – but it was difficult to think such as the hippocampus nickered musically and spun around him in a tight circle, stirring up the water with the haste of his passing. But the creature was far from going anywhere as his eyes gleamed, that slit opening up right at the base of his belly once again to allow the glorious slickness of his cock into view. Without thinking, Damien could not take his eyes off the beast, trying to spin and swivel in place underwater as the tightness on his lungs finally made itself known. Of course, his mind could have been a side kinder to him in allowing him to not think about the need to breathe in the dream but that was the whole hustling nature of their initial liaison, letting him know that he was in need of something more even while he failed, completely and utterly, to take what was right there before him.

"Come back!"

At least, that was what he tried to say, the throbbing, pulsing nature of that cock drawing his own to a rise, clothes tight and blood pumping. He couldn't think, most certainly couldn't breathe, but he had to try to follow, mouth open for the lure of the hippocampus' cock even as he spiralled away with a burbling laugh that spoke of eddies and waterfalls in his mountainous, watery home.

Not this time…

And then the water sucked back, a roaring fall that swept the beast up and away with a screech that could not have come from the lips of any natural animal, Damien reaching for him to no avail as he did each and every time the dream came to him. He could scream and shout, water trickling down his throat and up his nose in an unstoppable stream, but there was nothing just the one man could possibly do when all was beyond his control, the creature of myth and legend carried away as if he had never been.

Come find me.

A command or a request: that one was up for debate as Damien sucked in a breath, shooting upright in bed as if he had actually been trapped underwater. He slicked his hair back with two hands, surprised to not find it damp, and let out a curse, the stubble on his chin betraying the need for a shave. He shook his head, muscles aching and stiff, and eyed the sliver of light slanting under the blinds, a casting line across his pillow that had, unfortunately, drawn his dream to an untimely end before it could even become interesting.

What did it mean that he kept dreaming of the water horse over and over again, his smooth tail seeming to flirt and call him in more and more each and every time he had the dream? The ache he felt for him, of course, could not have been denied even if Damien had the sense of mind too, but it was not as if, either, he had spoken of his erotic liaison with the creature to anyone else. Why, they would have laughed at him at best and sent him off to a doctor at worst, although he doubted he could actually be forced into a medical situation against his will for something so ludicrously small. He was a man, however, who knew all too well how cruel human beings could be when they were drawn under the lure of doing something for the supposed good of someone else. And sometimes what was good for a man wasn't quite what the public thought should be good for him.

That was one of the reasons he'd ended up hiking alone in the mountains with only the view for company, ploughing on that time even though he'd progressively got himself more and more lost. Damien groaned, rising as he forced himself about his morning routine, laying out clothes for a job that sucked away a little more of his soul with every second he was present, remembering another time where he had gone and laughed carefree, his life much lighter for having fewer worried and responsibilities. Wasn't that the way of it though? One had to face trial and responsibility to find out just who they were and, of course, to work to live also. He couldn't just beg off from life chasing down a dream that the back of his mind wasn't all that sure about to begin with.

Yet sometimes one had to forgo what was normal and sensible and oh so mature too in lieu of something altogether more divine. His hand found his phone without the consent of his mind and he lifted it to his face with a dry mouth and eyes that stared off into the distance, vacantly open to suggestion. And he so very wanted to be suggestible, if it only meant that a little more adventure would come back to colour his life.

"Hi, Maverick, I'm sorry but I won't be in today. I've come down with a virus."

He knew where he needed to go.

*

It was a relief to allow himself back into the welcoming arms of the mountains, the skyline cut through with a jagged slice of cliff rather than yet another high-rise block of flats or office block. What affliction did man have with the earth that he continued to tar it? Despite working in central London, Damien sucked in greedy lungful after lungful of fresh, crisp air, lighter in heart and soul for being far away from what made his life tick around. He had to work but they would do well enough without him for a few days even if the pay would be sorely missed by his bank account.

No matter! He had to stride on, leave the little train station and delve into the heart of the mountains, his backpack and tent hitched up snugly on his shoulders. He was not foolish by far and had, at least, well-prepared himself for a trek that promised to be difficult on his body and soul but would prove to be a great deal more refreshing than any coffee or stint in the workplace.

He would find the hippocampus, the thought driving him on as night fell and he cooked over the campfire, eager only for dawn and the continuation of his trek. The temperature chilled his bones but he huddled in close to his sleeping back and trusted his knowledge of the mountains, however gleaned it may have been from books, to keep him safe, a quick breakfast fuelling him on his trek come the light of the next morning. It did not matter that he was unkempt and dishevelled and entirely in need of a hot shower, only that he sated the burning need in the depths of his soul, what drove him on each and every day since the beast had graced him with his presence.

And then, three days into a hike that threatened to be called to a halt with the low lying fog sweeping down and down into the cup of the valleys, he found the lake, the shimmering depths of a glacial lake left from a retreating glacier many years ago calling him down as if it had merely been waiting on him to appear in all the months that had passed. He caught his breath and stumbled down to it, loose stones and left behind debris sliding precariously underfoot as he skidded and scraped and cursed just like the first time, only eager to see just how he could turn his dreams back to a fitfully delirious sense of reality.

If he'd been more with his current version of reality, however, Damien may have realised that the fog should have dulled the glimmer of the lake, sweeping in so thick and low, but it didn't seem to cling to the surface of the water at all while still allowing bright sunshine through. That was just one of the many ways in which the lake was special and not least because it housed the creature who had called to him so beautifully ever since. For what else could he possibly put his dreams down to when he yearned for the cool embrace of a creature who should never have existed and yet, inexplicably, did?

Damien crouched, breathless, at the edge of the water, right out on the outcrop of rock from which he had first tried to spot the beast. He had no name with which to call him and hovered there awkwardly, eyes alight with intent that he did not have the knowledge to exact.

"Um…" He hesitated by the water, bag dropping heavily to his side and fingertips absently stirring up the surface into broken ripples. "Um… Are you there?"

What a silly thing to say but there was not exactly anything one could pull from a book for that kind of situation. He could have shouted, could have cupped his hands to his lips and hollered for the companion who should not have left him so soon, but he could not see that doing any good as he swallowed a curse and stalked back and forth, pacing the edge of the water like a caged tiger in the confines of a zoo.

Yet how was he to call out the water horse when he did not speak the silent language of the beast? Damien muttered something that could have been considered unpleasant to one in the know and kicked a rock: an entirely pointless and fruitless procedure that made him feel not a single bit better for all the effort he expended.

Well, if the hippocampus was not there, he would have to bring something to lure him out and Damien was sure that dried jerky and cheese wasn't going to appeal to his finer palate. With that goal in mind, he slowly swung about on his heel, reluctant to leave the lake even if he had something, however tenuous, in mind.

I thought you would not return to me, Damien.

He held his breath, blood pounding and roaring between his ears as he turned, so very slowly laying his eyes on the creature who he'd wanted to see every day since his first, divine, glimpse. And he was right there, his head poking from the water as if he'd been there all along and had merely been waiting on just the right moment in which to reveal himself, eyes glistening wetly as he shook his head, a dark mane that seemed, in the light of day, part fin laid slickly down the grey arch of his neck.

"I…"

But he couldn't get the words out and merely settled for kneeling down at the water's edge, right where the sand sloped into the lapping edge, two elements colliding seamlessly.

"You're here," he finally said, settling for the simple. "You really are here."

Of course, this is my home.

Damien should have expected such a snarky response, however plainly it was delivered, the hippocampus' words curling into his mind as if they were, indeed, born of his own thoughts. And it simply felt *right* to have them there, tickling at the back of his mind as if they should have always been there, just like the hippocampus had every right to be just where he was. Snorting droplets of water, he shook his head, mane flopping wetly from one side of his neck to the other.

Damien *grinned*.

"Mate, you have no idea how many of my dreams you've taken over, my days just thinking of…"

He swallowed hard, cutting off his own words abruptly as he coughed and rubbed his throat, a hot flush searing up his throat and cheeks as if he had been taken unwell all of a sudden. It was hard to say anything at all with a lump so large in his throat that he briefly wondered if his Adam's apple, perhaps, had doubled in size.

A fit of fever may as well have undertaken him as the water-equine surveyed him through eyes that seemed a whole lot more intelligent than many of the human beings that had had the ill-fortune to step into the swathe of his life.

"What..."

Yes, I did call you.

Damien inhaled slowly and deeply, concentrating on just how his breath felt expanding his lungs. It was hardly an answer, to an unspoken question, that he had not imagined before. It was, however, more settling to his mind to know that he wasn't completely and utterly barking mad.

"Oh..."

Did he dare ask the why of it or was that just *why* his mouth was so dry? Regardless of how many times he licked his lips and sucked his teeth, a terrible habit that his mother had tried many a time to get him out of, nothing he did softened the metallic taste in his mouth, need and curiosity battling with one another as his dream flashed before his eyes. It was not the place and most certainly not the time but one could hardly forget just what they'd done with the water horse last time they had come to the beast's lake and the creature himself knew that too. The hippocampus' eyes gleamed and he rose up a little more from the water, slicking and slapping his body down on to the sand-like dirt at the edge as he became a land mammal like Damien, at least for a time. Sooner or later, he would have to return to the chilly embrace of the lake but that was not something that either of them needed to worry about for the moment with a comfortable kind of tension fluttering in the air between them, tangible in its presence.

It was how it was meant to be, clear and simple, like being out in the wilds of the mountains with the city so very far behind him. Damien knew that that had never been where he was meant to be but it was the sort of life he'd fallen into, simply searching for a job, when there was so very much left out there to be experienced.

And…maybe…a sort of intimacy too. Even if it was not what any man could have ever expected, of course, but that was the beauty of breaking from the desired norm in that one could find things that they never knew existed.

The water horse's nose brushed his arm, nostrils fluttering sweetly with each and every breath, and Damien held his breath, remembering just how that touch had felt before, so solid and so very real. He could never have disputed that the creature existed but would have preferred to dote on his glory and praise him instead, even if such sweet words were not usually ones that leapt to coass lips and a working tongue.

The time for words isn't now.

Damien blinked. Ah, how did he know? But two of them could play that game – not a game, not really, but more of a dance that set his heart racing, a deeper need than he could have anticipated rising up anxiously in the pit of his gut.

"What?"

We can speak later.

The water horse's foreleg, fin and all, teased over his leg, a closeness that could only be matched by the feeling of being home on a cosy evening with a decidedly human lover, but where was the sense in rejecting someone just because they were not quite what he'd expected? Oh, how his heart *pounded* for the hippocampus, the mystical air drawing a rise to his crotch he would otherwise have been ashamed of if not for the fact that surely the hippocampus was a male and would, of course, understand his predicament. Laughing awkwardly, Damien rubbed the back of his neck and angled his gaze away, although all he'd wanted to do was lay eyes on his temporary lover again for the last several months.

Yet there was one thing amiss, one little thing that would too allow him to rein in his control, just a little bit.

"You..." Damien shook his head slowly. "This is going to sound mighty strange but...what is your name? I don't think I even asked you last time..."

Although that could have been seen to at a later time, he swore the creature smiled. But he wouldn't have to refer to him as a nameless being for much longer and that would render the sweetness of their lakeside interlude all the more divine for the revelation of it.

Gawain.

Nothing mattered from that point on, although the two of them could not kiss as those of their own species could. There was no sense of inequality between them as their lips came together, Damien tenderly cupping Gawain's cheeks as he trailed them over his rapidly drying for. And the water horse could not hold himself back either as his tail slapped the ground, driving a dent into the mixture of well-draining sand and stone, his desire well and truly told. No one had to hide what they were in his world, after all, although he was one of the very last of his kind – as Damien would come to know – but Gawain still had his own lusts and needs to be fulfilled.

Companionship, however, was one of the highest order. And that was just why he'd allowed Damien to find him again – nay, even *hoped* that he would find him again.

Moaning into the kiss, as tentative and exploratory as it was, Damien trembled against the creature, holding him and running his hands down his neck, exploring what he had been too struck dumb to do during the course of their first liaison. It was hard for him to worry about shifting his weight, hiking trousers tight around his crotch and upper thighs, as the grit and stones dug into his knees, caught up in the moment as he melded his lips, very gently, to Gawain's, eager for every last little one of the things that he had dreamt about for so very long in the twisted turmoil of his own bed.

I missed you…

Damien's heart leapt but he could not reply, only gasp, as the hippocampus' shaft eased out, slick and hard and self-lubricating against his stomach. It was impossible to miss, even if he had been attempting some sense of politeness and decorum, although the nature of their encounter was such that everything moved on naturally as the fog rolled and roiled up the slope from the glacial lake, secluding them off from view even though there were not any prying eyes about. But it was just the two of them and Damien grunted thickly, his hand slipping down Gawain's body as if it was moving of its own accord. And yet he could not have denied it was his own mind behind it as he grasped the hippocampus' cock smoothly, the fleshy spire tapered to a point that simply made his mouth water.

I have to…

That thought was not one that belonged to Gawain, however, Damien letting out a little whimper unlike anything that had ever before broken the barrier of his lips. But it was okay if it was for Gawain for the water horse could claim every last wicked part of him, everything that he would have been embarrassed to show anyone else, and so very much more too.

Gawain pulled at his shirt, speaking without words, and Damien obliged, blushing as his shirt was removed – what would Gawain think of his human body? He could not have been as refined as one of his own kind, surely, but the hippocampus nuzzled and lipped at his exposed chest, wriggling seemingly with happiness on the sand as he encouraged his human lover too to slip down his trousers.

It was difficult to resist the wiles of a creature with such imploring eyes and ticklish touches, lips pulling at his belt even as Damien's head swam giddily. Ah, but it was still very much a relief to free the hard shaft of his cock into the open air, despite the chill, and the touch of the hippocampus' lips wrapping around just the very tip drew a moan to his lips that he would have otherwise found himself ashamed of. He had been the one to take Gawain's shaft deep into the back of his mouth last time, barely able to fit what would have been a colossally large shaft on a human body but fitting the shape of the hippocampus' body perfectly; Gawain seemed determined, blissfully, to return the favour.

And what man would have gritted his teeth and pulled away with such a warm, soft mouth massaging the length of his cock? Slipping down, Gawain's muzzle seemed to suck in and pull around the length of his shaft, the hippocampus' own cock jerking and twitching, spurting pre-cum, as if he simply could not control himself in the meantime. Drifting as if in a dream, Damien groaned, although, to him, he opened his mouth and made no sound at all, so far gone was he already in the realm of lust. There was nothing for him in the world anymore but the hippocampus who had commanded his thoughts and dreams for so long, set on bringing him into a world where everything may very well just become lighter, warmer…altogether *brighter* than it had been.

"Gawain…"

The hippocampus drew back and nickered, tail flicking out into the water as he slithered back.

Join me.

He could have said no but, with his heart in his mouth, Damien bid himself to follow, hardly even feeling the chill of the lake water on his skin. How could he be cold, after all, when his love – at least, that's what he *hoped* the hippocampus could become, if they were not there already – beckoned him so sweetly, stoking the fire of lust in his heart while they swam and danced together, one more gracefully than the other.

Ah, but such sweetness had to be tasted as the hippocampus boldly rubbed the length of his body up against Damien, the man's breath catching. There was no way for him to be mounted in the water like one of the hippocampus' kind, but they could mosey to that outcrop of rock and let him grip it, the slick and slippery water horse's cock grinding up between his rear cheeks as droplets of water beaded and cooled on his exposed skin.

"Gawain!"

That time, the hippocampus' name came out as a moan that rose up from the back of his throat, a lustful sort of sound that he could not have claimed to have ever made before with any lover. For the hippocampus' cock was perfectly designed to tease open a willing anal ring and he plundered Gawain's tight passage, treating him as gently as a virgin as he kissed and licked softly at the back of his human's neck as he bore in, slowly and sweetly.

Relax…

The thought came tinged with a moan and Damien could not help but arch back into the hippocampus' thrust, as slow and gentle as it was, coaxing him deeper and deeper until he was spread and stretched out more than he could have ever imagined, the full length of the creature's cock seated within him. Right where it belonged, it twitched and spurted, filling him with a hefty dose of pre-cum as if he needed further lubricating, but Damien was already hot and ready for his hippocampus and all the pleasure he had to deliver.

There was nothing frenzied or rushed about their liaison as they moved together, Damien trusting Gawain to, at least somewhat, support him with his legs kicking a little wildly beneath the churned up disturbed surface of the water. It was up to the hippocampus, well and truly, to take control and thrust, dominating him so sweetly and blissfully that it was all too easy for Damien to slip into the submissive role, his anal passage ploughed and plundered by a shaft that he may have before wondered about its fit and size. But there could be nothing better for him than being stretched out by a kind lover and Gawain was all that and more, nuzzling at his hair and huffing hotly as he flung a foreleg up over Damien's shoulder, using him as leverage to buck and thrust as the water frothed softly.

But even a creature such as Gawain, oh so denied, could not hold back as the heat of the moment drove him on and on, grunting and snarling like the feral he was as he thrust harder and faster. There was only so much force he could put into his thrusts with the weight of the water and Damien's position working, unduly, against him, but that wasn't going to stop either of them as he unknowingly drove his cock up and over his human lover's prostate with each and every thrust, the tapered tip seeming to press so very sweetly into it that Damien simply could not stop the dam from bursting within him.

Yet, as the man moaned and rocked his hips through his orgasm, semen mixing with lake water to dissipate, Gawain let out a bellow that could only have come from an otherworldly being, slamming in with particular force for just a single thrust before spending every last drop he had to give. He had no balls held externally but he shot spurt after spurt of thick cream into Damien, filling him hotly even as trails trickled out to disappear as if they'd never been. But that vanishing act was vastly unlike what was developing between the two of them, two hearts coming together who had never really ever been meant to part the first time.

A frenzied, hasty orgasm came with its own kind of bliss as Gawain's still-spurting cock slipped from Damien, the hippocampus drawing him on to his stomach and tucking him carefully between his front legs. Exhausted in the afterglow and with a pleasant kind of soreness radiating out from his private passage, all Damien could do was collapse against him, his lover warding the chill off from his bones as he tenderly cradled him close.

I'm glad you came back.

Damien could not have put to words just how he felt about the hippocampus, chuckling breathlessly to think that he had only met him twice – and, of course, had engaged in sweetly sexual acts both times. If he had met a man in the bar and done the same with him, he most likely would not have thought anything of it but there was something different about the warmth of the hippocampus pressed against him as he drew him out into the lake, lying on his back to support Damien on his stomach and chest.

Sculling gently, Gawain let them float in the afterglow, cock soft against his sweet's stomach, his eyes half-closed. In such a position, it was all Damien could do to not slip into dreamland himself, holding on to the moment at all costs, but he had nothing to truly fear about losing his newfound friend and lover for a second time.

No... Gawain was going to do everything he possibly could to persuade him to stay.

That was, if Damien would have him, of course.

Lake Monster's Lust

The mountains had called him from the city, though Ben still thought, sometimes, that he was just a city boy thinking that he could say something to the wilds, the wilderness and snowy mountaintops that called him so. Sure, there was snow, sometimes, down in London, but there was only so far that brown slush under the wheels of yet another red bus could take him.

His hair was pinned and flattened under a mustard-coloured beanie hat, though it was curling around his ears, in need of a trim. It was always pretty much in need of a trim when it came to him, though he didn't mind too much. He was an artist, working in the city, though he never really came out to the country where he had been brought up, where he had been born in the middle of Wales.

It was strange to him, stubble on his jaw, not needing the office-smart suit and tie that so many did down in London, the pace of the city relentless, even at times when the world and the country was naturally meant to be slowing down. He was glad of that, though the business of the city did move him along quickly, too quickly. Wasn't there something about artists needing to take things more slowly? Or perhaps that was where the idea of a starving artist came from, working for little, slow, lazy…

He'd never wanted to be lazy, but he needed a break too, confused where he needed to be clear. That was why Ben was out there in the mountains, looking down into the bowl of a glacial lake, so clear, so blue. Of course, that was only the reflection of the sky, not a cloud to be seen, though the wispier, lighter ones higher up in the atmosphere were visible, just about, if one squinted.

That was good. He liked needing to look a little bit harder, to see what was there. That was what he hoped to bring to life with his artwork.

But what he could not have imagined was having the very nature of what he did, on a day-to-day basis, challenged on his visit to the Welsh mountains that day. It had just been meant to be an overnight trip, but it would end up being so very much more than that as a ripple in the water caught his eye.

At first, he wondered if it was a fish, or perhaps a small school of them, though he had never considered what kind of mountain fish might have been present in a lake like that, formed during the retreat of a glacier many years ago. He wished that he could have been there to see the majesty of the glaciers, though he would have to go overseas to Iceland or another place entirely to see the rivers of living ice, moving so subtly that the human eye could not detect them, yet alive and flowing still.

It was a good thing he had his sketchbook in his backpack, in that case, halfway through his trek and eager for a break, even though the sun was high in the sky. He needed a moment to spend his time there, slipping easily down a gentle slope, littered with pebbles that could have been pushed there many years ago before the glacier retreated. It was a shame Ben could not remember the name for it, but Ben did not need to.

Not as the monster of the glacial lake reared their head, nostrils flared, smooth, slick skin beckoning his eye. He blinked rapidly, rubbing the back of his hand across his face, though that did not change anything, not as he grunted and stumbled, shocked in the brightness of the sunlight.

They were there… As if they had been there for many years already, their head lifting, something rippling down their neck. For a moment, Ben thought they were a horse, though they were so much more than that, a creature who had stepped right out of the books of myths and fantasies, bringing light to a side of life and the mountains that Ben had never considered before.

"What are…"

He tried to talk, but the words stuck in his throat, thick and cloying, snarling up there where he could not force them out. Ben's mouth opened and closed, eyes fixed on the creature, yet the curl and slap upwards of a thick tail betrayed the creature's true nature.

"No…"

The beast's eyes locked on to him, the lake monster surveying the intruder into his domain. With a long, thick tail and a fluke at the tip, he was strong, powerful, all that he needed to be. He had a pair of forelegs still, though they came with wide fins that better allowed him to scull through the water, moving fluidly with it, as much a part of it as any being that spent their entire lives in the water could be.

They swam closer, Ben stumbling back, fussing with his feet, not knowing truly whether he wanted to move closer or further away. It was a monster, surely… Yet he could not hold back his innate fascination for it, something that had his heart pounding, leaping, thrusting its way up into his throat and staying there.

A dream… or not. He didn't know. But he knew that he had to know, kneeling at the edge of the lake and a wide slab of rock that could have been slate. He'd heard there were lots of slate mines still in the area, though they were quite often boarded up.

He swilled his hand through the water, though the creature stayed out of reach, watching him, floating back and forth. Ben licked his lips, his mouth suddenly too dry, watching the monster's tail sweep from side to side, slowly, through the water, hypnotic, spellbinding.

Had his life changed forever? Well, that remained to be seen.

"I must be dreaming…" He said to himself, though the words slipping from his lips were not ones that he truly believed. "Heck… No one is going to believe me."

He would have taken a photo, but his fingers shook too much to get his phone out of his pocket, ignoring it, slumping down on to his legs in a sort of sitting position, legs stuck out to the side, before the lake. The cool slab of rock warmed to the heat of his body, though that could have been his hammering heart that made it heat up so quickly, feeding on him looking for something greater.

The water horse swam up, a monster of the lake, mottled with pink and blue and green, their skin slick and shiny with the water that flowed seamlessly over them. A ridge of fins ran down their neck with a fin on either side of their head too, where their ears would have been. If ears were present on the monster, however, they were not to be seen as more than soft indents before those ear-fins.

"Who are you, human, to disturb me here?"

What? He blinked. Sure, the water horse's lips had moved and the voice had come as if it had bubbled forth from under the water, but…well…it didn't sound right.

Of course, it didn't sound right, he told himself. That was because a creature couldn't talk! Yet who was he to say what was real and what was not, what could be and what could not be, when there was a real to life myth and legend swimming in the water before his eyes? Everything that Ben had thought he'd known regarding the natural world was a lie and there was nothing he could do to change that.

"Are you going to say anything, or are you going to simply sit there and stare at me? Isn't that still considered rude, even for humans?"

The monster's voice was lighter and more teasing than Ben could have imagined, chortling a soft laugh as he shook his head. He watched the beast's head lift from the water, that long, strong tail sweeping back and forth under the surface, shaking his head again and again.

Ben couldn't help but laugh as the water horse frothed up the water into a bubbling churn.

"What are you doing?"

The beast paused, if only for a moment.

"Playing with the bubbles. Maybe if you did that more, you wouldn't have to stare at me and wonder what I am. Hm?"

Ben considered that for a moment, running his fingers back through his hair, the backpack slipping off his shoulders. It didn't seem to belong there any longer.

"Right, um… Yeah… Sorry?"

"Oh, no need to apologise, you're the first person I've seen here in three years," the creature replied smoothly, swimming all the way up to the shore and resting their chin on the slab of slate. "It's nice to see someone again, especially a human that doesn't run screaming. And you are a male too…if I see things correctly."

"Yes, yes, I am," Ben confirmed, though he chuckled shortly. "Wow, I didn't think… Hm, I don't really know what to say here. This is all new to me… Do others know you're here?"

If the monster could have shrugged, he would have done so.

"Perhaps. No one that troubles me has come looking, which is more than enough for me. I am Dafydd, though my partner has been gone for many years, Gawain, only myself in here. Who are you?"

Ben blinked.

"Um… Me… Yeah… Yeah, I'm Ben. You can call me Ben."

"I like that name. It's easy to remember."

Dafydd sculled back and forth in the water, the wiggle of his tail helping him stay afloat, though it was as if he did not have to expend very much energy at all to move through the water or even to drift. The water ebbed and flowed around him, though Ben could not help but notice something on his belly as he rolled over, exposing a paler underbelly and a little more of his mottled skin.

"Er… You…"

The fact of the matter was that the lake monster's slit, if that's what it could be called, was parting slightly, allowing his length to show. It could not be determined as anything other than a maleness, though there was a need there too that had Ben stuttering back and blushing.

"Yes?"

It was as if Dafydd knew exactly what he was doing, allowing a curved shaft to slip free of his body, though Ben tried to respectfully avert his eyes. It did not feel right, no, not at all, though he thought his eyes shouldn't have lingered as long as they had otherwise. Surely the water horse just saw his body differently, the hippocampus not a creature but a being as intelligent as human beings. Maybe even more so.

He swore Dafydd was laughing at him, however, as he stuttered, stumbled, tried to find the right words to continue talking.

"Look, mate, I'm not sure what I'm doing out here or if you're even real yet," he confessed, laying all his cards on the figurative table. "This is strange… People don't think that hippocampi, like you, exist. I still don't know. How do I know you're real?"

Dafydd shot him a look, swimming in close and rolling on to his back to show off his shaft again, a foreleg waving with the long, slim flipper teasing through the air in a drip of water. Ben gasped subtly, yet it was enough for the water horse to take his chance.

"Well, you can touch me. That might convince you that I'm real."

Ben's words choked in his throat.

"Um…" He shook his head. "Maybe if you put that thing away first… That's weird. Well, I mean, surely perfectly natural, but people don't go around with their dicks hanging out, that's all."

"Am I distracting you?" The water horse said with something that could only be deemed a tease, his tail flicking up, though he did keep his shaft hidden, if only for a moment longer

"I wouldn't have thought a man would be so easily swayed. Then again, it has been some time since I have been able to seek pleasure with another."

Ben raised his eyebrows, his face decidedly pink, though he hoped Dafydd didn't notice. *Dafydd…* He sounded the water horse's name out in his head. It was a pretty name, a soft name that ended on the "eeth" note, though that was his tongue butchering it a little. He tried to mimic, even in his own head, how the hippocampus had said it, though it was harder than he might have expected.

Maybe he could get him to say it again?

"Um…" He realised he had not said anything for a while, Dafydd still staring at him, something pulled between them, tension unspoken, crackling, teasing. "Yeah, maybe. I'm not used to that."

"Well, as I said… Touch me, you'll soon find out I'm real. You hardly seem disgusted or repulsed. That's usually a good start when I find a human like you."

He shook his head, though he smiled along with the water horse's bubbling mirth. It was infectious, in a way, though he didn't need to say any more than what had already been said. It might not have been a moment Ben had been expecting to see that day, but it would have been rude of him, surely, to not allow the hippocampus to lead where he willed.

Truth be told, he was a little hot under the collar too, though that was not something Ben would be able to understand for himself until a lot later.

Not everything had to be explained straight away, however. That was okay too.

A flicker of desire pulled at his stomach and he shook his head more slowly as Dafydd lifted his tail from the water, brushing it over Ben's legs, which were still slumped off to the side. Probably going numb by then, but he hardly dared move. Maybe it would break the spell…

"What do you say then, human Ben?" The water horse teased. "I think I'd like this… It's an open invitation and you are curious. Could this really be that bad for you? It's been such a long time since I had my dear partner and no one has ever given me any relief, no one I have met here…"

"Well, I…" Ben licked his lips, blushing, hardly able to believe what he was about to propose. "I could help? You know? Must be hard to get relief like that…you know, having flippers and all? Humping through, like, moss and stuff…"

Dafydd blinked at him, though the water horse's head picked up, tail sweeping back and forth in a motion that Ben could only take to be excitement.

"I did not believe that you would come over to my way of thinking so swiftly there," he teased, though he was too keen for things to progress to hold back, slipping closer to the edge of the water. "Why don't you come a little closer then?"

Ben swallowed. What?

"Your interest is clear..." The water horse coaxed him closer, flipping his tail, sculling on his back. "There's nothing that's going to go awry here... When are you ever going to have a chance like this ever again?"

Flushing, Ben shook his head, pressing his hand to the back of his neck. It was warm, unduly so.

"Erm... I guess...not?"

Yet something pushed him on, as if an otherworldly force or higher power, if he believed in that sort of thing, was urging him to try. He had spent so long doing what was expected of him and it seemed like he was done with that.

It was somewhere no one would see him, yes... Nothing could go wrong?

"You're not going to drag me into the deeps, are you?"

Dafydd chuckled and winked. The monster actually *winked*.

"Not unless you don't give me release... That was said in jest, I promise!"

The laughter, however, served to ease a little between them, the tension that had sparked and crackled unduly. It helped, a little, that Ben did not have to slip out of his clothes at all, his backpack set aside, the monster slipping up on to the rocky shore, the smooth pebbles there lifting his hide so that he was supported. A creature of the water like Dafydd did not seem as graceful up on land as he could have been, his forelegs resting out before him like flippers as his tail twisted to the side.

But that exposed his cock all over again, the slender length with the curve in the middle. Ben tried not to think too much, though it was hard to do anything else as his heart pounded terribly, his skin prickling, body aching in a weird and wonderful way. He wanted it, his curiosity up, though his shaft hardened too, tucked away in his hiking trousers. They were not tight enough around the crotch to hide his need, though he hoped that the water horse was not as focused on him as he had originally thought.

"Tell me if I hurt you…okay? This is…weird."

Dafydd trembled as the man's hand closed around his shaft, stroking it lightly, though it was almost slippery under his touch with its own mild, gentle lubrication.

"Mmm… Oh no, that is divine… It is almost like my sweet mate is here again, with me."

Ben could not be quite sure what that meant, but the moment was right and he relaxed into it a little more as he ran his hand up and down that length, feeling out the curve, the pressure of it fitting nicely into his hand. It was interesting, but in a way that had his breath hitching and catching in his chest, even though Ben had not thought it should have been the sort of thing that got him turned on. It didn't make sense, but there was no longer all that much there that made any sense at all, not as he allowed his mind to soften, to drift away.

If he only thought about what he was doing, giving pleasure, enjoying the moment, he didn't have to worry about anything else. He only had to be there, in the moment, his hard-on pressing through his hiking trousers, the bulge obvious, though only to him. The water horse was too stretched out with his lips parted and nostrils fluttering to know and care, grunting softly.

"Oh… Oh, yessss…"

It was a good sound to hear, knowing that he was causing pleasure, that he was bringing them to a state of being that could not be gleaned in any other way, even though it was very much not what Ben had thought he would be doing on going into the mountains that day. But that was fine, just fine, as the fires of his own lust were stoked and teased to a burning crescendo, wanting to remove his clothes even in the fresh, crisp air and yet not daring to.

Not then. Not yet. Maybe another time, a day coming soon, that day... Oh, Ben could not keep his thoughts straight, not as the monster, who was very much not a monster, grunted and groaned under his touch, trying to rock into his thrusts. Dafydd might have had more muscle and flexibility to him than Ben initially gave him credit for, for he was able to thrust and grind as smoothly as if they were both creatures of the land, though Ben could never see him as quite like a human partner.

"Unff..." The water horse groaned. "Oh... Yes... Yes..."

It must have been good for him, though Ben did not dare ask, licking his lips, adjusting his position yet again to hide the spire of his cock from showing through his trousers. He didn't understand why he was so hard, why his body felt as if he had not cum in months, desire coursing through him, throb after throb, spilling pre-cum even into his own underwear. What the hell was up with that? He wasn't a teenager and had not been for years, yet he found himself lusting for the water horse with the smooth, otherworldly member with the curve in the middle like a lustier, more needy being.

Maybe it was one of the reasons why he had felt pushed to please the hippocampus, Ben thought dimly, the thought swimming through a haze of lust simply to make it somewhat to the forefront of his mind. It didn't make sense, didn't have to make sense, not in the glow of the sunshine, the brightness of the day that did not quite seem to match up with the sordidness of the act taking place there. The smooth "schk" of his hand moving back and forth along Dafydd's cock filled the air, pebbles shifting against one another while the hippocampus' tail swept back and forth. Even he could not contain himself, though it was not as if Dafydd had been asked to restrain himself in the slightest.

"Mmmph," Dafydd groaned, appearing a lot less refined, his skin drying faintly, revealing lighter shades and textures. "Yes... Please... More... So close..."

That was about all the warning Ben got as he pumped the hippocampus' cock all the more fervently, caught up in the motion of giving him pleasure, though he was too far gone in his own aroused passion to care what he was doing. It felt good and Dafydd wanted him to keep going – so what the hell did any of the rest of it matter? Ben groaned deep in the back of his throat, his blush creeping down his neck, pumping and teasing lustfully until there was nothing the water horse could do but to release his pleasure.

It came in a frenzy with no more words of warning, though Dafydd's tail lifted and his nostrils fluttered in a high-pitched whinny as he spent his load. It poured forth from him in long, powerful spurts, as if his body was trying to drive every rope of cum, a slick sheen to each, into a partner, as deep as possible. Dafydd's body did not understand how it didn't have a partner to thrust into, not quite at that moment, only that pleasure swamped it, the water horse's eyes falling half-lidded in swimming lust.

The spurts went on for longer than Ben could have anticipated, spattering the monster's stomach, painting the stones, even some of it splashing into the lake where it immediately dissipated. Yet there would be a memory of the lust shared there in the aftermath, regardless of how quickly the water sought to wash it away, the monster's skin warm to the touch under his hand, cum glistening.

"Oh…" Ben sucked in a breath. "Wow… Just…wow…"

For there were no other words to describe what he saw, the prickling, tingling lust in him that clawed at the pit of his stomach like being with no partner had ever done for him. Dafydd raised his head with a glitter in his eye that had not been there before, a fin twitching, though the man could not read what lay in his expression. That was something that one could only glean after time together, even as his hand remained curled lightly around the water horse's cock. It was as if he didn't quite realise that the moment was done, that he had given Dafydd everything he had asked for, the man still wanting…something.

Snorting softly, Dafydd ducked his head, the frill running down the back of his neck quivering wetly.

"Maybe there is something more we can do for each other…"

Watching the throb of the hippocampus' cock spilling more cum over his belly, trickling and oozing, Dafydd swallowed hard. His cock ached.

"What did you have in mind?"

For his time with the water horse of the lake was not yet over…

Thank you for reading and I hope that everything was very much enjoyed!

Ready for more? Check out my author website for more furry fiction and where you can purchase my books!

https://linktr.ee/amethystmare

Cover art illustrated by verysweetpotato; they are contactable via Twitter for work enquiries.

twitter.com/AlexandrCorvin

www.ingramcontent.com/pod-product-compliance
Lightning Source LLC
Chambersburg PA
CBHW030025200726
48283CB00012B/1016